THIS THING OF OURS

Gladys Cross

This Thing Of Ours

Copyright @ March2021
Written by: Gladys Cross
ISBN: 979-8724455145

Editing: Revision Division, Kimberly Hunt
Cover Art: Meryl Pierce Designs
Special Thanks: Amber Szklarski and Meghan Redlin

AUTHOR'S NOTE:

This Thing of Ours is a dark mafia romance, and may contain themes and subject matter that might offend sensitive readers. You can expect to encounter violence, murder, death, profanity, kidnapping, explicit sexual situations, suspense, crime, and characters with questionable morals. Reader discretion is advised.

ONE

RACHAEL

"I had a vision," my grandmother says over the phone.

"I assume it's about me."

My teeth bite into my lip as I move away from the middle of the sidewalk.

"A wolf with chestnut fur runs through the forest, jumping over logs, and splashing through streams. Catching the scent of his mate, he pushes himself harder. He stops at the edge of the forest and looks across the clearing. Only it isn't a female wolf I see, but you."

"That's a good sign though, right?" The brick building I'm standing in front of has a row of windows along the side and I lean against one of the casings as I try to piece together what has my grandmother on edge about this vision. "Seeing a wolf in the forest is a sign of good luck within our tribe."

"I'm not so sure this time. The wolf raises a paw to step out from the cover of the forest, only to set it back down. Looking around, he sniffs the air, sensing danger. He stands there, letting out the eeriest howl I've ever heard."

"I don't understand your vision, Grandma."

Shifting positions, I look up at the blinking diagonal neon sign for Mel's Place.

"I'm not sure what it means yet. In time, I'll figure it out. How are things in the big city?"

"After working hard all day, I'm finally unpacked. I didn't feel like cooking, so I thought I'd walk around the block and see what restaurants are close. I'm sitting on a ledge in front of what appears to be an old-fashioned diner. I wasn't expecting to stumble across one of those here."

"Why am I not surprised you're settled after only two days? You never could stand anything out of place. Go eat. Let me know how the food is."

"Miss you already. Give everyone my love."

Hanging up, I push off the ledge and head inside the diner. At this hour, there aren't many people in here. A man wearing jeans, a biker's vest, and a bandanna over his bald head sits on a stool at the large center counter.

As I slide into the booth, I watch the woman a few seats down from him. Her dark brown hair is in a tight ponytail that falls just below her shoulders and her formfitting khaki pants showcase a slender build. She's partially turned toward the back of the diner where two men sit across from each other in a booth by the restrooms. The way she swivels toward the counter, then swivels back to face the men, makes me think she's watching them.

The man facing me is handsome, with short dark hair and beautiful olive skin. His tie has varying shades of gray and blue to match his light gray suit.

Chestnut brown hair brushes along the top of the dark royal blue suit jacket of the guy sitting across from him. His hands drum on the table as he speaks, calling my attention to them. They're rough and callused, which seems out of place. His clothing says Wall Street, but his hands say construction worker. As I stare at his long lean fingers, I imagine how they would feel trailing along my neck toward my breast.

"What can I get ya, hon?"

"Huh."

She pushes her graying hair out of her face while resting her hand against her ample hip. "Are you going to order, or sit here all night with a blank stare?"

"Tuna melt with fries and a Coke, please."

She takes my menu, walking toward the men sliding out of their booth. When they head toward me, I get my first look at the guy who'd been facing away from me.

His lips make a perfect bow, with the top lip being thinner than his full lower lip. He has just the right amount of facial hair; more than a five o'clock shadow, but less than a full beard. The slight dip on the bridge of his nose suggests it's been broken at some point. When he nears my booth, he slows down and stops right in front of me before calling out to his friend.

"Christian, I'll be out in a minute," he says, his voice smooth and even with a distinct Brooklyn accent.

The other man gives him a nod and heads out the door.

"Mind if I join you?"

Staring into eyes a shade of blue so dark they almost look black, I nod. He slides into the booth, resting his left arm along the red leather back while his other hand drums on the gray Formica table.

"My name's Giovanni Moran."

He sits there watching me, as if I should know who he is. As I study him, I notice the frown lines on his forehead, and I wonder what he looks like when he smiles.

"Am I supposed to be asking you for your autograph or something?"

"I'm not used to people not knowing my name." He chuckles. "Everyone calls me Vonni. You're not from around here, are you? I would have remembered seeing you."

"I just moved here." Leaning forward, I put my elbows on the table, supporting my head with my joined hands. "I'm curious. Why would you have remembered me?"

He looks thoughtful for a minute, like he isn't sure if he's going to give me an answer.

"In my line of work, reading people is…. Essential. You can always tell a person's intent by their eyes. You have the warmest and most beautiful brown eyes I've ever seen."

"Huh, usually I get hit on for either my boobs or my ass. Eyes are a new one."

"I noticed all of your features… after the eyes, of course." He drops his gaze from my face to my chest and back up. "What's your name?"

This man is dangerous for me. Not that I think he would ever lay a hand on me. More in the way he makes me feel. Like a cat who wants to rub up and down his length.

"I'm still deciding whether I'm going to give it to you."

"Why?" His brow lifts. "You already know my name."

"You seem like the type of guy that doesn't get told no often."

"You could say that," he says, his lips lifting on one side.

Leaning back in the booth, I toy with my napkin sitting on the tabletop. My eyes alternate between his lips and his eyes, and I decide to take a leap of faith.

"My name is Rachael."

He turns his head to look out the window. The guy he sat with earlier leans against a large black SUV parked at the curb with a phone against his ear, motioning for him to hurry.

"Shit, I have to go." He takes his phone from inside his suit jacket and slides it across the table toward me. "Give me your number."

Convulsively swallowing, I stare at it for a minute before I add my name and number to his phone. When he takes the phone back, his hand runs along mine, causing a tingling sensation to shoot from my scalp down to my toes.

He slides out of the booth, leaving the restaurant without a word. Looking out the window, I watch his powerful stride as he approaches the guy leaning against the SUV on the phone. The guy smirks at Vonni before heading around the back of the vehicle to get in on the driver's side. Vonni pauses at the open door and winks at me before turning to get into the passenger's side.

A minute later, from inside my purse, my phone chimes. Digging around inside its voluminous pocket, I finally locate it and pull it out before it stops ringing.

"Hello."

"I just wanted to make sure you gave me your real number," Vonni says, his smooth voice causing goose bumps to break out across my skin.

He seems like he's always in control and a perverse part of me wants to mess with him a little. See if I can't get under his skin.

"Who is this?"

He coughs and sputters before answering. "How many men have you given your number to today?"

"Only one so far, but the night is young. Just out of curiosity, what would you have done if I had given you the wrong number?"

"First off, you made me choke on water. Second, you won't be giving your number to any other men. Third, I would have made Christian drive around the block and come back. To make sure you stay out of trouble, I'm taking you out to dinner tomorrow. Text me your address and I'll come for you at 6:30."

"Are you crazy? I'm not giving a strange man my home address. You could be a serial killer."

"Fine, I'll text you the name and address of the restaurant, and I'll meet you there." His voice drops an octave. "There are lots of things I want to do to your body, all of which I very much want you alive for. See you tomorrow."

Staring down at my phone, I sit there for a minute. Slowly, the sights and sounds from the diner come back to me and the server appears to hand me my food before walking away in a huff.

The girl in the khaki pants stands there staring at me

for a moment after she pays her tab before shaking her head and heading out the door. Could she hear our conversation? What's up with this girl? First her interest in the guys, then me, and there's no common denominator that I can figure out.

Looking out the window, I watch as the woman in khaki pants walks over to the biker guy standing at the curb. The lines of his face are harsh, and she makes wild gestures with her hands. Now there's a bizarre duo if I've ever seen one. His eyes meet mine as he continues to argue with her. He glares at me before grabbing her arm and yanking her out of sight.

TWO

VONNI

"Never thought I'd live to see the day," Christian says, smiling in my direction as he tries to focus on the road.

"I assume you have a point."

I send him a dry look, knowing it won't shut him up.

"Vonni Moran asking a random broad out on a date." He gives me a sideways glance. "What's different about this girl?"

"I told her my name, and she had no fucking clue who I was." I shake my head and laugh. "She asked if she should get my autograph or something."

"She's sure as shit isn't from around here."

"No, she said she just moved here," I tell him, running my hand along the scruff on my jaw. "She eye fucked the shit out of me when I was standing right next to your pretty ass. Then she wasn't sure she was going to give me her name. I thought she gave me a fake number."

"Would you make me drive back around chasing some broad?" he asks, raising his eyebrow.

"I sure as shit would. You owe me. Do you know how many

calls I've fielded for your ass this week alone?"

He barks out a laugh, pulling up across the street from a run-down cement building. We sit there for a minute watching the three men that are milling around the outside. In our line of work, it's not wise to jump out of the car on this side of town without getting your bearings.

"Did DJ say he's still inside?" I ask, as Christian lights a cigarette.

"Yup." He blows spoke through the side of his mouth. "You want me to text him?"

"No." I nod my head. "What do you make of the guy hanging out to the right of the front door?"

"Hard to tell from this far away. The other two are crackheads, for sure. My guess is they got run off when they spent all the money they had."

"Let's get this show on the road, then. Go in after me and hang back."

Getting out of the car, I shut my door, heading across the street. My eyes scan back and forth as I walk. The neon sign above the battered white aluminum door shadows the face of the man I asked Christian about in contrast. He doesn't move a muscle as he looks at me, so I give him a nod and open the door. There are no streetlights outside, which is a good thing because lord knows nobody wants to see who's coming or going from this establishment. The interior is even more gloomy, and I let my eyes adjust as I stand just inside the door.

I'm stopped by a tall, leggy blonde as I move toward the bar that runs along the right side. She runs her hand up my chest to my shoulder, batting her eyelashes. It escapes me why chicks think that will get them somewhere with me. By the spark of recognition in her dull blue eyes, I can tell she knows who I am. Funny, innocent brown eyes with long lashes are my new obsession.

Letting my eyes wander down the length of her frame, I stop at her tits, covered only in a few strings with flowers over her nipples. Her surgically perfect globes don't have the usual effect on me. In my mind's eye, I see a blue shirt stretched across natural full tits that look as though they would fit perfectly in my hand.

"I don't suppose you can help me out with something?"

"I'll help you out with anything you want," she says, rubbing her tits against my arm.

"Perfect." I lean down to speak against her ear. "I'm looking for a guy that went back to a private room a short time ago. Heavier set, real hairy, dark hair. Ring any bells?"

She meets my gaze. "What's it worth to you?"

Reaching into my suit jacket, I take out a large wad of folded bills, pulling out two hundred-dollar bills and holding them between two fingers just out of her reach.

"Will this get me to the exact door he's behind?"

"Follow me," she says, before sauntering away, her hips swaying as she walks.

When you get out of the primary room of the club, it looks more like dingy office space than private rooms in a strip club. The gray carpet looks like it's at least twenty years old. Each door we pass looks the same, except for gold numbers on the white doors. Halfway down the hall, she stops, nodding her head at number six. She holds her hand out expectantly at me with a smirk on her face.

"Thanks for the help," I tell her, pushing the folded bills into her hand and watching as she turns around and heads back the way we came.

Lord, I hope the damn door isn't locked. Pulling my gun from its shoulder holster, I open the door. This room is more brightly lit than the hallway, even with only one bulb blinking in its fluorescent light. When my eyes land on Leo, I soon wish for poor lighting. The popping sound the stripper makes as she releases his dick and looks over her shoulder at me causes the pancakes I had earlier at the diner to turn in my stomach.

"Leo will no longer need your services." I keep my gun at my side, knowing better than to holster it around Leo. The girl makes no move to get off her knees. "You heard me, beat it."

Between the gun and my tone, she scrambles up from in front of the worn brown leather couch, walking as fast as her legs will carry her out of the room. With a wave of my hand, I indicate his nakedness.

"Put your dick away, we need to talk."

I shut the door, never taking my eyes off him. He stands, pulling on his tighty-whities and jeans, careful to keep his hands where I can see them. Donning his worn white T-shirt, he sits back down on the couch. There's a small round table with two plastic folding chairs tucked under it and grabbing one, I sit down.

"You want to talk, so talk," he says, leaning back as he crosses his arms over his chest.

"Let's cut to the chase. You're in for thirty grand. I've sent Sebastian by twice now to collect, and all you do is pay enough to bet again. I can handle this one of two ways. Let you end up in the landfill and still not get a dime out of you or send you on a job that clears your debt."

"Don't sound like much of a choice, does it?" He leans forward and smiles. "What do you want me to do?"

"What you do best, of course. I need you to lift a 1967 Shelby Mustang GT500 and have it down at the docks by Tuesday." Pulling a slip of paper out of my pants pocket, I hand it over to him. "Here's the container number where you'rc going to park it."

"You don't ask for much, do you?"

"There's always the landfill, Leo." I stand up, pushing the chair back under the table. "Until your debt is clear, there's no more betting either. I've already put the word out with the other families." With a glare in his direction, I back out of the room. "I'll see myself out."

THREE

RACHAEL

Coming awake with a start, I hear someone banging on the front door. I reach for my phone on the antique blue nightstand, realizing it's already after ten. The banging continues, so I jump out of bed and make my way down the hall to the front door. When I open it, I come face to face with a stranger wearing one of the most interesting outfits I have ever seen. Before I can even process his getup, he comes inside the apartment and starts looking around.

I cross my arms over my chest and ask, "Can I help you with something, or did you just come to browse my apartment?"

He's so busy looking around the living room that he takes a moment to respond.

"Girl, don't get all crazy. I need to borrow brown sugar to finish making my breakfast cookies. Since I'm here, I thought I'd look around on account I'm nosy."

He moves into the kitchen, opening cupboards and looking inside. I try to decide whether I'm going to make coffee for the two of us or call the police.

He's only a few inches taller than me, which is odd given I'm so short. His makeup is tasteful, showing off his flawless mocha skin to perfection. Long fake eyelashes are at odds with his hair, which is shaved close to the scalp. A red blouse falls off one shoulder, and leopard print leggings are tucked inside his blue cowboy boots. A feather boa in the same shade of blue as his cowboy boots hangs around his neck. Even if I take a chance of ending up on the news, he's too interesting for me not to know.

He closes the cabinet door under my sink, where I keep my cleaning products. "You have the most well-organized kitchen I've ever seen."

"OCD has its advantages. I'm Rachael, by the way." I take the coffee can down from the cupboard above the coffeepot, turning to him. "You want to stay for coffee?"

"My name is Dave, but I prefer to go by my stage name, Chantal. I'll just run back to my apartment to mix my cookies really quick." He grabs the brown sugar from the counter and winks. "They can cook in your oven while we're having coffee. Be a doll and set that baby to 350."

He sashays through the kitchen and out the front door. Starting a full pot of coffee, I leave him a note and head for the shower. If we're going to have a long chat session, I prefer not to do it in my robe.

Twenty minutes later I emerge looking less like something that was drug out of a trash can, to find him on the couch watching HGTV.

"Ray, this Bailey's creamer is to die for." He pauses, raising my mug with a picture of a kitten with the saying *hang in there* to his lips. "Where did you find it?"

"I've only been to the small family-owned grocery store a block over. It's all I can muster with so much to do before I start work."

He sets his coffee cup down to follow me into the kitchen, grabbing an oven mitt out of the drawer by the stove. His nosing around has paid off.

"The key to my breakfast cookies is the jam. They are actually healthy, but we won't tell." With one hand full of hot cookies, he pulls a hot mat out of the same drawer and sets the cookies down. "The cookies have to set for five minutes before we dig in."

"Yes, sir. Which show were you watching?"

"I can't get enough of Joanna Gaines. That girl is fierce."

"I agree with you." Pouring creamer into my coffee cup that says *I love to wrap both hands around it and swallow*, I smile at him. "You know what. I think we're going to be the best of friends."

He waves his hand, snapping his fingers as he says, "Gospel."

We move back into the living room and watch another episode while we're waiting for our cookies to cool. After the episode ends, he disappears into the kitchen and returns a moment later with a plate full of cookies covered in jam. Setting it on my emerald green coffee table, he sits back down on the couch next to me.

I bite into the cookie and moan.

"Damn, this is good."

"If we're going to be best friends, I'm going to need some backstory," he says, biting into his own cookie. "I haven't seen you in the building before."

"I'm from a small town a few hours north of here. The type of place where everyone knows each other, and none of them mind their own business. I got married straight out of high school and for several years, everything was fine. Gradually, I noticed changes in how he treated me. Then my cousin Kevin told me his flavor of the week saw him with another woman. Come to find out, it wasn't just one, so I moved in with my cousin Bobby. Eventually, I got tired of seeing him around town with different women while he was trying to get back together with me and decided I needed a change."

He shakes his head. "Men can be assholes."

"Your turn," I say, folding my legs underneath me and settling in.

"Where to start." He taps his chin. "I suppose I've always known I was gay. In high school, I began wearing women's clothes."

"You have a stage name, so I'm guessing you're in drag shows?"

"Yes, darling. I work at an elite club downtown bartending in between shows. Until last month, I had a boyfriend. It was devastating when I caught him stealing the money I had set aside for rent. If I'd had to ask my mom for money, it would have been humiliating."

"Are you from around here?"

"All my life." He sighs. "I've never even traveled."

"I've been around New York state, but that's it for me too. I had to use my savings to move, so my bucket list has been put on hold. It was worth it, though."

"I'm working tonight. You should come see my show!"

"I can't tonight." My cheeks heat at the image of Vonni that comes to mind. "I have a dinner date."

"Do tell." He sets his plate on the coffee table, leaning in. "You've only been in town for two days and already you have a date?"

"An unwise date."

He gives me a once over. "When's the last time you got laid?"

I grimace. "Two years."

"Two years? What the hell for? You're practically a virgin again. Jesus, Mary, and Joseph!"

How to explain my insecurities? If he's going to be my friend, he might as well know me in all my messed-up glory.

"Now I know what I'm about to tell you isn't logical, but here it is. I wondered if he had to go somewhere else because I was so horrible at sex. After a while, when there's nobody you want to have sex with, you quit caring about it. Then

17

yesterday, out of the blue, I had sexual fantasies about a man's hands. He's the first guy I've thought about in that way in a very long time."

He opens and closes his mouth as if he's trying to decide how to say what he's thinking.

"You need to sleep with the man you met yesterday in order for you to see for yourself that there's nothing wrong with you. We are going to get off this couch and get you a sexy outfit for your date. That way you go into it feeling good about yourself."

He stands up and holds out his hand. There is a distinct possibility he's right. At some point, I'm going to have to face my fears. Since I'm starting over, there's no time like the present. He has me halfway out the door before I realize I don't have my purse or shoes.

Not having any idea where he's taking me, I dutifully walk next to him. After we've walked three blocks, I feel the need to ask some questions.

"How far is this place? This isn't some never-ending quest, is it? I do have a car."

He rolls his eyes. "I know a guy who can help us another block over."

Stopping in front of a small red brick boutique with an ornate wrought iron hanging sign, he holds the thick oak door open for me. Once we're both inside, he takes my hand and leads me to the middle of the store.

The man standing behind the long oak counter is tall and trim, with jet-black hair, and a thick seventies mustache complete with lamb chops. His psychedelic print silk shirt has varying shades of pink and purple tucked into snug black jeans. When he catches sight of Chantal, his face goes from looking like he just swallowed a Sour Patch Kid to a brilliant smile.

"Chantal, darling, what brings you by?"

"My new BFF has a date tonight. I need a full workup. Sexy, but classy. We want to get laid, but not scream streetwalker."

He nods, coming around the counter to give me a complete visual inspection.

"Turn around."

Feeling ridiculous, I do a full circle. When I dare a look at Mr. Sourpuss, I expect him to find me lacking, but I'm surprised by the smile on his face.

"You may call me Rico," he says, extending his hand.

"Pleased to meet you, I'm Rachael." Shaking his hand I ask, "Do you think you can help me with a look for my date tonight?"

"Of course. By the time I'm done, you won't even recognize yourself."

Turning on his heel, he hastens toward the back of the store and my short legs have me running to keep up. He moves from rack to rack, grabbing clothes so quickly I can't tell what he's grabbing. The man doesn't even know my size, yet he has an arm full after only flitting around the store for a few minutes.

"Try it on one at a time and let me see," he commands, dumping clothes onto a brown leather bench. "I may need to make some adjustments to what I picked or the size."

"Thank you."

My stomach churns as I tuck a low-cut black silk blouse into a formfitting electric blue pencil skirt and do a turn in the mirror. Instead of being self-conscious, I feel sexy. When I emerge from the dressing room, I strut around, both men giving me a once over before nodding their approval.

"Put that in the yes pile and try on the next one," Rico says.

After trying on twelve outfits, I end up throwing four into the yes pile. I justify the other three outfits to myself with the excuse that I'll wear them to work. My dress for tonight is a glittery silver formfitting number with the back cut out to the top of my butt that Rico insists on pairing with silver stilettos.

"Thank you so much," I tell Rico, kissing him on both cheeks as he hands me my bags.

At the door, he reciprocates by embracing me before we

leave. On the walk back, Chantal entertains me with funny stories about wig mishaps and eye makeup failures at the club. One thing about my new bestie, he'll never be boring. As we climb the stairs, I wonder what time it is.

"Oh my god, it's 5:30!" I look over at Chantal in horror. "I only have an hour to get ready."

"Get in the shower," Chantal says, taking charge of the situation. "I'll put everything away while you're doing that. Then makeup."

By the time I come out of the bathroom wrapped up in a white fluffy towel, he's sitting cross-legged on my bed with makeup spread out next to him.

"Where did you meet this guy?"

Sitting next to him, I close my eyes.

"I went to the diner a few blocks over for a late dinner yesterday. On his way out, he stopped by my booth and asked if he could join me. When he had to leave, he asked for my number. To tell you the truth, I'm not sure why I gave it to him. He wanted to pick me up for dinner, but I hardly know the guy, so we agreed to meet at the restaurant."

"I'm done, go look in the mirror."

Getting up, I go into the bathroom to examine his handy work. Makeup has always been too much of an effort for me, however I can't argue with the results. My eyes have that smoky look you only see in magazines.

As I stood there, he came at me with a lash curler, and I cringed. The effect, however, is amazing. He's taken my naturally long eyelashes and made them look thicker. My lips are the color of a merlot wine, complementing my tan skin to perfection.

"What are you looking for?" I ask Chantal as I watch him rifling through the bathroom drawers.

"Mousse, dry shampoo, hair spray, something along those lines."

"I have dry shampoo in the top right drawer."

He pulls it out, spraying my hair before searching for a

blow dryer. Between the blow dryer and a round brush, he arranges my short locks in pretty waves around my face.

"Now hurry and get dressed. I'm dying to see the results of my efforts."

Standing in front of the mirror, I feel sexier than I have ever felt in my life. My hips sway with a sensual flare that would rival any supermodel as I walk out into the living room for Chantal's inspection.

"Oh girl, there is no way he's not trying to hit that."

He switches from teasing to serious. "I think you should let me drop you off at the restaurant. Worse case, the date is terrible, and I pick you up before I head into work. Best case, he takes you home and ravishes you. In which case, I'll expect a full report. Of course, I'll be jealous that you got laid, and I didn't. If you drive yourself, it makes it a little harder for him to make a move."

"You make a valid point. If you don't mind, I'll take you up on that offer."

FOUR

VONNI

The sound of gunfire rings out as I walk past my sister to take my place in the stall next to hers. Clipping my target in place, I press the button to send the carrier out ten yards. I load the magazine, release the slide, and take aim before firing off all thirteen rounds. Next to me, I hear Mandy rapidly firing off her own rounds. It was her idea to come here this afternoon. She thinks if I keep my skills sharp, it will keep me from getting shot. Life doesn't work that way, but I humor her, anyway.

By the time I've gone through all the magazines I brought with me, Mandy's no longer in the stall next to me. Clearing the last magazine, I make sure the gun is empty before setting it down. When I turn around to look for her, I catch sight of her leaning against the cement wall. She smiles, yelling to be heard over my protective earpiece.

"I'll walk out with you after you clean your gun."

I quickly dismantle my gun, cleaning all the parts before I put it back together and slide it into the case. The need for a case at all is an amusing farce. Once we get out to the parking lot, I'll just reload it and put it in my shoulder holster.

Mandy leads the way through the range, passing about twenty stalls before going through a set of steel reinforced doors. Macy leans against the counter in the gun shop, her long red hair spreading across the glass. Her tits are on full display, damn near spilling out of her tank top. When she sucks hard on her lollipop, Mandy makes gagging noises next to me. Smiling over at my sister, I wave to Macy on our way out.

Our cousin Christian fucked her last year. When he failed to call her back, she slashed his tires. Our brother Rafe thought he'd fare better. He found out he was wrong after having to ice his balls for the day. Neither of them will ever learn.

From across the parking lot, I spot Sebastian leaning against Mandy's cherry red BMW 3 Series. Mandy's car is her baby and having Sebastian lean against it will set her off, which he knows. They have been bickering back and forth since she turned fifteen.

Sure enough, she doesn't say a word, taking off across the parking lot toward him.

"What the hell, Seb!" She stops dead in front of him, crossing her arms over her chest and gritting her teeth. "You don't own it, so don't touch it."

"Are you saying your precious car can't take my weight?" To mock her, he leans back farther. "If that's the case, then don't drive it, princess."

"You know I have a gun case in my hand, right?" She smiles sweetly at him, which is never a good sign. "I'll just pop off a couple rounds in your classic Charger."

Sebastian straightens up, knowing better than to test her. She is a Moran, after all. With a smile he does, however, muss her hair up as he brushes past her to stand next to me. Shaking my head, I watch my sister fix her hair before sticking out her tongue at him.

"What are you doing here?" I ask him, knowing gun ranges have never appealed to him. He's more apt to use his fists or a bat.

He smiles and claps me on the back. "Christian and I went out to breakfast this morning."

At this moment, I want to punch Christian in the face.

"So." Mandy looks between the two of us. "I don't get what that has to do with anything."

"Vonni has a date."

Sebastian rubs his hands together, waiting for my response.

"Like an actual date, not like an arrangement with a hussy?"

Sebastian laughs hysterically while I give my sister a sideways glance.

"Christian and I had time to kill while we were waiting for DJ to locate Leo. We stopped at this diner to grab something to eat and when we got up to leave, I saw her in a booth and stopped to talk to her."

Mandy's mouth hangs open, and Sebastian quickly leans over to close it.

"Details, dear brother, details," she says, slapping Sebastian's hand away.

Christian will pay for this.

"What do you want me to tell you?"

"If Sebastian hadn't come along, you wouldn't have said a word. Twin ESP is totally not a thing. At least with you it isn't."

She smells blood in the water, so there's no point in avoiding the inevitable.

"Fine." I give her a look of displeasure, which, of course, does me no good. "She's hot, and I caught her staring at me even though Christian was standing right next to me. I don't have to tell you that shit never happens. And she had no clue who I was." Maybe telling Mandy would serve one purpose. "How do I keep her from finding out?"

"You don't fucking carry tonight, I'll tell you that right now," Sebastian says.

"I can't believe I'm going to say this." Mandy shakes her head. "I agree with Sebastian. You need to call DJ."

"Why not me? This is a job for his best friend."

"No offense, Seb, but you're a big guy. You kind of stick out in a crowd and he needs someone that can blend in. DJ is perfect for that job." Opening her car door, she points at me. "I expect a full report at dinner tomorrow."

"My work here is done." Sebastian grins, stalking off toward his car.

"You're an asshole, you know that!"

He just waves at me over his shoulder.

FIVE

RACHAEL

Picking at the sequins of my dress, I look out the window as Chantal drives me to the restaurant. He does his best to make idle conversation to distract me, but gives up halfway there.

The car slows down, so I pay closer attention to my surroundings and spot Vonni's lean body against the red brick exterior of the restaurant. A decorative black awning partially blocks my view of him, and twinkle lights strung around the shrubbery by the front door cast a subtle light that's not enough to lift the shadow covering the part of his face I can see.

"See the guy wearing a charcoal suit with a black shirt open at the collar?" I lean back against the seat so Chantal can see around me. "That's him."

"I can tell just by looking at him he can throw a girl around. You might not walk for weeks."

His teasing has the desired effect, and my nervous energy leaves me as I laugh. Getting out, I go to shut the door, but

Chantal catches my attention by raising his hand.

"Remember, if you need an out, text me."

"Thanks, bestie," I say with a smile, shutting the door.

When Vonni catches sight of me, he pushes off the wall and walks toward me. His purposeful stride falters as he gets closer. The way he stands there watching me with such concentrated purpose reminds me of a predator stalking its prey.

"You look sexy as hell." His accent thickens as he says, "Are you sure you don't want to just go home and order in?"

"You promised me dinner to keep me out of trouble." I give him a shy smile from under my lashes. "Going home with you definitely constitutes trouble."

He touches so low on my back that he's almost touching my butt, and the heat from his hand warms my entire body.

"I meant trouble as in you with other men."

His breath near my ear causes the hair on my arms to raise. What in the world is wrong with me? Walking through the thick wooden door of the restaurant, I give my eyes a moment to adjust to the dimly lit brick interior.

"Mr. Moran, I didn't know you were going to be dining with us tonight." The maître d' nods in my direction. "Who is this lovely lady you've brought with you?"

"Angelo, this is Rachael." He moves closer, sliding his hand up my back, stopping between my shoulder blades. "You'll be seeing her with me from now on."

"Very good. Right this way," he says, turning on his heel and leading us back into the restaurant.

On our left, a group of middle-aged men sit in a dark brown leather booth smoking cigars. Several of them stare as we walk by, one of them inclining his head ever so slightly in our direction. Vonni's hand remains warm on my back as he guides me forward, following closely as we pass a handsome older couple sitting at the small solid oak bar on the right. The woman smiles at me while the man nods at Vonni.

Angelo stands off to the left in a private alcove, with a

chair pulled out in front of a round table draped with a black tablecloth. Vonni moves his hand from my back around to my hip, drawing me flush against him, stopping me from sitting down.

"I've got it, Angelo."

With a nod, he retreats to his domain. Vonni releases his hold on me, moving behind my chair to pull it out. He pushes in my chair, brushing his hand along my bare arm before taking his seat in the overstuffed chair to my right.

He leans back in his chair, his body partially turned to the side so that he faces me. His right hand rests on the table, while the other casually lies across his leg. My eyes are drawn to the hand resting on his thigh. Swallowing, I notice he sits with his legs spread apart. My gaze moves to the hand drumming on the tabletop, and it takes a moment for the sound of his voice to register.

"I hope you like Italian."

If I'm going to focus on what he's saying, I need to quit watching his hands, so I look at his lips.

"I love pasta."

Big mistake. My gaze moves up to his eyes.

The server interrupts before Vonni can respond. "Mr. Moran, what a pleasant surprise. Who is your lovely friend?"

"Colin, this is my girl, Rachael," Vonni tells him, his eyes never leaving mine.

"Lovely to meet you, Rachael."

I give him my brightest smile, happy for a distraction from Vonni's eyes and lips. "What wine do you recommend?"

"Do you prefer red or white?"

"I love both. Surprise me."

He turns to Vonni. "And for you, sir?"

"I'll have whatever you bring her."

With a curt nod, Colin leaves the table, disappearing into the kitchen.

"Everyone seems to know you. Do you come here often?"

There is a long pause, as if he's trying to decide how much

he should say.

"I own the place."

Leaning forward, I rest my head against the knuckles of my right hand. "Do you own other restaurants as well, or just this one?"

"I own various businesses with different members of my family. This is the only restaurant I own, though." He shifts in his seat, as if he doesn't want to talk about what he does for a living.

Returning with our wine, Colin sets it in front of us, along with the menus.

"Do you know what you want?" I ask to buy myself some time as I glance at the menu, hoping my eye will fall on something delicious.

"I'll have the seafood Alfredo," Vonni says without looking at the menu.

I suppose when you own the place you don't need a menu.

"The same for me, please."

Colin collects our menus before turning on his heel and leaving the table.

"Most girls only order salad."

"I'm not a size two, so there's no need to pretend." I clasp my hands over my mouth, regretting being so blunt. "My mouth gets me in trouble. I just say whatever pops into my head."

"I love that you're not afraid to say what you think around me." He gives me a cocky grin. "As for your body, well, there's nothing that doesn't turn me on about it."

A swig of wine buys me some time while I try to think of something to say. When Colin drops off a basket of bread, I tear off a piece, stuffing it in my mouth.

Vonni clears his throat. "How do you feel about Mexican or Asian food?"

"There's nothing I don't like in either area." I swallow, noticing that he stares at my throat as I do. "If I were to pick favorites from each category, I'd say chicken chimichanga and

Vietnamese noodle soup."

"We have similar tastes in food." His gaze moves from my throat to my lips as he plays with the stem of his wineglass. "I can't say I've ever had Vietnamese, but I love Chinese, Thai, and Japanese."

"Vietnamese noodle soup is like their version of chicken noodle soup. The noodles are clear rice noodles, and the veggies are different. Normally, it has various leafy things that I don't ask about. All I know is it smells delightful and tastes like heaven."

"I will have to trust you on that until I can try it for myself." Vonni starts to say something else, but Colin dropping off our food makes him pause. Once we're alone again, he rolls noodles around his fork and asks, "What do you do for fun?"

"Like hobbies or what I do when I'm not working?"

"Both."

"On weeknights I like to veg out in front of the TV or read. On the weekends, I love to be outside. Hiking, camping, or just sitting on the lake. Occasionally, I go dancing with my cousins. What about yourself?"

"I like to make furniture or refinish pieces. When I'm not doing that, I like to watch movies at home. I've never been a wonderful dancer though, and I don't get outside the city very often."

His hobby explains the callused hands I've been fantasizing about.

I watch him from under my lashes. "So you're saying you're good with your hands?"

"I'll let you be the judge of that."

The illicit promise of his words causes a shiver to go down my spine.

"Do you have a big family?"

"Yes. Nonno is an only child, but Pop has two sisters. Ma has four sisters. All of them loud and nosy. I have a twin sister, two younger brothers, and tons of cousins."

"Nonno?"

"It's Italian for grandfather." He gives me a lopsided smile. "Nonno is from Naples and insists everyone learn Italian."

"My great-grandmother had twelve kids, so I have tons of cousins as well, but my grandmother only had my mother, and my mother only had me."

"Twelve, huh?" His eyes go wide, and he blows out a breath. "Can you imagine having that many kids?"

"No, I can't imagine having that many kids. But that's what people did back then on the farm. Now it would be hard to have a family that size."

He cocks his head to the side. "If money were off the table, how many kids would you want?"

"Three kids, preferably boys."

"Why boys?"

"Don't let the makeup fool you, my friend did it for me. I'm not a girly girl. My only real nod to femininity is wearing dresses and getting my nails done. I wouldn't have any idea what to do with girls."

"You just moved here." His brow crinkles. "Which friend did the makeup?"

"I met my neighbor today. He did my makeup, took me shopping, and dropped me off."

"You'll have to thank him for me, particularly for the dress."

He leans to the side, ogling me. My insecurities creep up and I grow nervous under his watchful gaze. My eyes wander, looking for something to bring my attention back into focus. They come to rest on the hand by his thigh, but before I can get myself into too much of a fluster, Colin returns. He's quickly becoming my knight in shining armor.

"Can I get you anything else?"

"No, we're all set," Vonni responds, never taking his eyes off me. He reaches into his suit jacket and withdraws a large wad of folded bills, handing him two. "Have a good night, Colin."

Vonni stands, offering me his hand. When I place my hand in his, he pulls me into a standing position. Not expecting him to be so close, I have to steady myself by laying a hand on his chest. Through the fabric of his dress shirt, I can feel the thick outline of the muscle in his chest.

"Let's get you home."

I'm feeling so out of sorts that all I can manage is a nod. He steps back, leading me by the hand through the restaurant.

Once we're outside, he stands still, scanning the street, before moving toward the same SUV I'd seen him get into before. He opens the passenger door, stepping back for me to get in. The SUV is high, but it has a step I can use and as I place my foot on it, his hand comes to rest on my butt, lifting me up. Once I'm settled, he shuts the door, coming around the front of the SUV.

"Look at you grabbing my butt under the guise of helping me in."

"You should get used to it. You have a fantastic ass. Where am I going?"

"It's the North Shore Apartments over on West Langdon Street."

"I know where that is," he says, pulling into traffic.

Settling into my seat in the dark interior of the car, I watch the scenery flash by. Only knowing Vonni for a day, it feels odd to be so at ease sitting next to him. He reaches for my hand as he drives, running his thumb along the top of my hand to the ends of my fingers. For the life of me, I can't understand how with such a light touch he has every nerve ending in my body humming.

At my apartment building, he lets go of my hand to get out of the car, and by the time I slide down to the sidewalk, he's in front of me. He puts his arm around me, pulling me into him, while he closes the door behind me.

We stand on the sidewalk with my hands on his chest and his arms around me. He leans forward, brushing his lips against mine, tracing his tongue along the seam of my lips.

Sighing, I open for him and his tongue sweeps into my mouth, brushing against mine. He widens his stance, sliding his hands down to cup under my butt, lifting me snugly against him. I rub along his length, trying to get closer, wondering what his skin would feel like against mine.

"Let me come inside," he groans against my lips.

He makes me shiver at the picture his words evoke. The streetlight illuminates his face and I see not only desire, but longing. Even if all I ever have is one night in his arms, I know I'll never regret it.

"I want you to come in, but I need you to take things slow. It's been a long time since I've been with anyone."

He keeps one hand on my butt as he walks next to me, guiding me toward the building. As we mount the steps to the outer door of the apartment building, he walks so close to me that our thighs brush. The entire climb up the three flights of stairs, his hand never strays from my butt.

"You really were serious about me getting used to you grabbing my ass."

When we reach the landing, I head for my apartment, digging in my purse for the key. Standing at my front door, I feel his breath on my neck just as I find my key.

"I want to touch every inch of you," he whispers in my ear.

My keys make a clattering sound as they fall from my hand. As he bends over to get them, he runs one hand along the length of my leg as he stands. Unlocking the door, he places his hand on my butt and pushes me inside the apartment.

He locks the door behind us and while I set my purse on the bar, he looks around the living room. Moving to the right, he peeks into the kitchen briefly before heading back through the living room and down the hallway. He gives a cursory glance inside the first room he comes to, which only has a TV and an elliptical in it, before proceeding to the end of the hall where my bedroom is.

He stops at the worn brown leather chair in the far corner,

sitting down to remove his shoes and socks, sliding both under the chair. I lean against my dresser, placing my hands on either side of me as I watch him. He stands up to remove his jacket, laying it across the chair. His hands deftly work the buttons at his wrists before continuing down his shirt, the muscles in his bare chest flexing as he reaches for his belt.

"How long is a long time, exactly?"

"Two years, give or take."

I stare at his hands while they go to work, unbuttoning and unzipping his pants.

"Why so long?"

He slides his pants down, throwing them on top of the growing pile of clothes. He's so distracting in only his black boxer briefs that I have a hard time concentrating on the question. His lean frame is thickly corded with muscle. Even his calves are thick and muscular. I've never thought a man's calves were sexy before now.

"There's been no one that made me want to." I go back to staring at his hands as he slides his briefs off, throwing them on the chair. He's now standing completely naked before me, and I try to finish my thought." Have sex, that is."

"I'm ok with you using me for sex." His voice is gravelly and his accent thick.

My mouth goes dry at the sight of him standing there with his hand wrapped around the girth of his penis, his abs flexing in time with the hand stroking up and down his considerable length.

"I don't want just sex from you," I squeak, surprised by my admission.

"Are you sure? Because you're staring at my cock."

"I'm thinking about how you might not fit."

Blushing, I bravely raise my eyes to his face.

"Cara, I'm just a man. We don't have to have sex if you're not ready yet." He stands in front of me, barely touching me. "I want to see you naked and spread out before me."

"Cara, what does that mean?"

"The Italians use it as a term of endearment."

He runs his hands down my arms to my side, unzipping the side zipper of my dress before pulling it over my head. I stand before him in nothing but black lace panties and silver stilettos. Hooking his thumbs in my underwear, he slides them down. While he's bent over in front of me, he slides off my heels one at a time, rubbing along the arches of my feet, as if he knew they had been pinching in these shoes the entire night.

He moves to the end of the bed, pointing down at it. "Lie on your back."

Curiosity eats at me as I move across the bed. Lying on my back, I find the courage to meet his eyes.

"Now I want you to spread your legs wide."

Awkwardness gives way to a feeling of sensuality as I notice the way his eyes drink in every inch of my body.

"Wider for me, cara. I want to see all of you."

My eyes travel down his muscled abs, stopping at the hand that has resumed stroking up and down his length. With my eyes on him, I bring one hand to each breast, cupping and raising them. He lets out a groan as I go from cupping them to gently pulling on my nipples. I let my hands wander down past my stomach to part my nether lips, leaving my core open to his gaze.

He drops his hand, crawling up from the bottom of the bed to lie on his side. His body touches the entire length of mine.

"You're so fucking sexy," he breathes into my ear before taking the lobe into his mouth.

Kissing down my neck, his hand moves from his side to cup one breast before taking my nipple between his fingers and rolling it, causing my breath to hitch. He bends his head to my other breast, licking my nipple before sucking it into his mouth, my body arching into him as he sucks.

His hand trails down between my open legs, teasing my slick and swollen flesh. Leaning on his elbow, he looks down the length of my body, watching his hand expertly stroking me. My hips have a mind of their own, moving against his rough, callused finger that only adds to my pleasure. Never taking his eyes off his hand, he increases the speed and pressure.

"I want you to come for me, cara."

His rough voice is commanding, throwing me over the edge. He continues stroking me long after my body quits shaking against his hand, wringing every ounce of pleasure out of my body.

"I want all of you." My voice sounds breathless and foreign to my ears.

"If you're not on something, I have to grab a condom."

"I'm on the pill."

I run a finger down his chest, watching the muscles twitch and move at my touch. He moves my hand aside so he can roll on top of me. His lips seek mine just as I feel the broad head of him at my entrance. He enters me part of the way and holds still, giving me time to adjust to his size, his entire body shaking with the effort. The spindles of my headboard groan as he grabs them, thrusting the rest of the way inside me. Wrapping my legs around his hips, I take his cock even deeper inside of me.

He breaks the kiss, panting against my ear. "Fuck, you're tight. I love how wet your pussy is for me."

My nails drag down his back, eliciting a shiver as he rocks his hips back slowly before thrusting into me again. My body is strung out, and I'm craving the release I know he can give me. I don't want slow and sweet.

"Harder."

He lets go of the headboard and sits back on his haunches, pulling me roughly to him. Holding my hips, he thrusts in and out of me hard and fast. The force of my climax causes me to shiver around him. With another deep thrust into me, his whole body shakes, and he collapses on top of me.

Utter contentment steals over me as his weight presses me down into the mattress and his breath ruffles the hair next to my ear.

"Damn, I don't feel like moving."

"So don't." I place a light kiss on his cheek. "I'm quite comfortable."

My thoughts tumble around inside my head as I run my fingers through Vonni's soft chestnut locks. He hadn't been faking his sexual attraction to me, and he damn sure didn't fake his violent release. I've been struggling with sexual self-doubt for a long time. It's bizarre to think that a one-night stand has me considering things I should have before.

What if my ex-husband's infidelity had nothing to do with what I did or didn't do in bed? An even crazier thought pops into my head. Could I have sexual prowess, after all? Lying there listening to Vonni's even breathing, I mull that last thought over before sleep finds me.

SIX

RACHAEL

Bright sunlight pierces through the blinds, and I find myself in a bit of a pickle with Vonni still sprawled across me and my bladder screaming at me. He looks almost angelic with his long lashes fanning his face, and I hate to disturb him. I try to shimmy out from under him but when his arm tightens like a coil around me, I know sneaking into the bathroom is out of the question.

"Where are you going?" he mumbles, his eyes fluttering open.

"Bathroom." I run my hands through his sleep tousled hair, kissing his forehead. "You're comfortable, stay in bed."

He lets his arm go slack, and I slide out of the bed, tiptoeing into the bathroom. As I look at my reflection in the mirror, I know I'm out of my league. I'm not a one-night stand girl.

What should I do? What's my next move? Furiously, I brush my teeth, deciding on a nice hot shower. At least then I'll be facing Vonni looking cute, instead of my hair standing on end and Chantal's makeup job running down my face. I get in and close my eyes, savoring the scorching water.

My eyes snap open when I hear the shower door and Vonni's standing there, his gaze intense, his blue eyes darkening to the color of a deep ocean abyss. He looks every bit as sexy as he did the night before, maybe even more so with his hair a mess from my hands running through it. Since he's staring at me already, I might as well give him a show.

His eyes follow the path of the soap as it slides along my body. He holds his thick cock in his hand, rubbing up and down its length while he watches me. I take my time soaping my nether lips. He lets out a groan when the water rinses away the soap and I slide a finger lightly along my clit. The water cascades down my curves as I continue to touch myself. While it's highly erotic to know he's enjoying the sight of my body, I'm itching to run my hands over his smooth skin.

"I want to soap you now."

His gaze fixates on my breasts as I saunter up to him. He turns us around, letting the spray run down his back. Soap in hand, I run it over his chest, working my way down his stomach, my hand teasing along his length before I cup his balls.

Setting the soap aside, I let the water cascade down onto him. All his muscles tense as I bend over, licking the broad head of his penis before sucking him into my mouth. As I take him all the way to the back of my throat, he cradles the back of my head with both hands. He lets out a strangled moan as I suck hard on him. When I lift my gaze to meet his eyes, he's openly watching me. Sliding my lips and tongue backward to his head, I suck gently before sliding all the way to his base. The muscles in his abs jerk and his breathing becomes more labored as I slide my mouth up and down his length.

Lightly, he runs his hand along my face, touching my lips before working a finger into my mouth. Dislodging my lips from him, he grabs my shoulders, drawing me up his body.

"Why did you stop me?"

I bit my lip, wondering if maybe I'm not doing as good of a job as I think I am.

"It feels fucking amazing when you suck my cock." His hard voice makes me shudder. "But when I come, I want to be deep inside you."

He turns off the shower, opening the door, and lightly pushing me out of it. We're dripping wet, but neither one of us cares. He grabs me, fitting my body along his as he kisses me. There's nothing tender in it, his kiss demanding with an almost desperate edge. Backing me up until my butt hits the sink, he lifts me onto it. His hand pushes the upper half of my body back, leaving me to support myself on my palms. Breaking the kiss, he grabs one leg in each hand, spreading me wide.

"Mine," he says, meeting my eyes before bending forward to lick my core.

He alternates between biting and sucking on me until I violently come, shaking and gasping. Keeping a hand on either thigh, he pulls me forward until I'm balancing on the edge of the sink and forcefully enters me. He moves in and out of me in quick, hard strokes, remembering from last night exactly how hard I like it.

Moving my right hand from the edge of the sink to his forearm, I use it to steady myself so I can sit up. My nails dig into his shoulders as I cling to him, wrapping both of my legs around his hips. He keeps up the pace of quick, hard strokes, making me scream his name with the intensity of my orgasm. Wave after wave of pleasure crashes over me. He cries out, throwing his head back. My whole body quivers at the sensation of his hot cum releasing inside of me.

Both of us are panting and clinging to each other. My hands move along his shoulders up to the nape of his neck, ruffling his hair as our breathing slows. I've never had such an intense connection with anyone before. I lean back, looking into his face, trying to figure out what he's thinking.

He opens his eyes, smiling down at me. With a sigh, he

lifts me off the counter, setting me on my feet. Reaching for a towel off the rack, I think he's going to hand it to me. Instead, he runs the towel over my wet head. He spends an inordinately long time drying my hair, before toweling off the rest of me. By this time his body is almost dry, so he opts for hastily passing the towel over his hair.

"What are you doing today?" he asks, folding the towel and putting it back on the rack.

"I don't have any plans. Why?"

"I have a family thing I have to go to. How about I come back for you at four?"

"You want me to meet your family?"

I stare at him with my mouth hanging open.

"They are a little much for anybody to handle."

He releases a breath he had been holding with a pained look on his face.

"I'm sure you're being dramatic. Are you sure they won't mind?"

"Are you kidding me?" He pinches the bridge of his nose. "My bringing a girl will be all anyone talks about for days."

"You don't bring girls home?"

"No. The type of girls that go for me aren't girls you want to bring home. They want me because of my family." A frown mars his handsome face. "I have a few things I need to get done at the house before I come back for you."

"Go ahead, I'll see you later."

With a quick kiss on the lips, he leaves the bathroom to get dressed. Following him out, I grab my robe from the closet, throwing it on before I search for coffee, pondering what he just revealed to me.

His family must be wealthy, or powerful. I'm just a poor kid from the reservation. What if I use the wrong fork, or wear the wrong thing? Vonni seems down to earth, but that doesn't mean they will be. My musings are interrupted by the feel of his lips on my neck.

"See you soon," he says against my neck, before heading

out of the kitchen.

I hear Vonni say from the front door, "Can I help you?"

"Well, good morning, handsome," Chantal replies, no doubt breezing right past him like he owns the place.

When I come out of the kitchen, I can't help but giggle at the look on Vonni's face. He's not sure quite what to do. Chantal, on the other hand, looks like a cat that just caught a mouse.

"Vonni, this is my neighbor Chantal. He's the one I told you about last night. He took me shopping and did my makeup."

"Help my girl any time." He claps him on the back, throwing me a look over his shoulder. "I'm sure I'll be seeing you around."

The moment Vonni shuts the door behind him, Chantal turns to me, and I know I'm in for it.

"Did boyfriend just call you his girl?" He gives me a sideways look. "Shit, the sex was hot, right? He's got that bad boy look about him. Shoot, he can spank me any day."

"I can attest to him not playing for your team. Besides, he's mine, and I have no intention of sharing."

"Is that so, Miss Thang? You better pour me a cup of coffee and tell me everything. Don't leave any juicy details out."

We sit on the couch with our coffee in hand while I relay all the details of the evening, finishing with him asking me to meet his family today.

"Meeting the family." He watches me worry my lip. "Are you nervous?"

"Yeah. It's more than that, though. I get the impression from Vonni they're of some importance. I don't know what I'm walking into or how to dress."

"Girl, leave it to me. Clothes, hair, and makeup are my specialty." He frowns. "This is a serious step for only having a first date."

"Vonni is a serious guy. It's like everything about our relationship keeps taking eight steps, instead of one. I thought I was only getting one night, but it appears I have a chance at more."

"And do you want more?" Chantal raises an eyebrow. "You just said relationship."

I don't know how to answer him because frankly, I'm still working through everything that's happened and all the feelings that go along with it.

SEVEN

VONNI

"Today was a Good Day" blasts as I skip down Rachael's steps. Digging in my suit jacket for my phone, I open the outer door to her apartment building. It's probably either Mandy or Ma expecting a detailed report on my date. Letting out a sigh, I look down at the caller ID. Shit, this is a bad sign considering I'll be seeing him at dinner tonight.

"Morning, Pop."

"Where are you off to?" he asks around the dinging from my car door.

"Home." I close my door. "What do you need?"

"Home, heh." He huffs out a sigh. "Maybe this news will get me out of the doghouse."

"I know I'm going to regret asking this." I pull out into traffic. "What does my date have to do with your being in the doghouse?"

"Your mother thinks I put too much pressure on you," he grumbles. "Something about grandchildren one day. She doesn't want to hear that I'm not getting any younger, and you need to be prepared to take over for me. But when I tell her you were just leaving her house in the morning, though . . ."

"I tell you what, Pop." Looking in my review, I take a quick right. "I'll let you be the one to tell her I'm bringing Rachael to dinner tonight, on one condition."

"Blackmail is a fine art, son."

"If you want to stay in the doghouse, be my guest." Even after my quick right, I notice the same red Honda following behind me. "It would be a shame, however, if I were to tell Ma the dating lecture you gave me when I was sixteen was the reason she's not a grandmother yet."

"Never have kids. They're a damn lot of trouble, and hell on your love life." He chuckles. "You're getting good, though. Almost brings a fucking tear to my eye. Now, wiseass, what do you want?"

"You're in charge of making sure everyone behaves."

When I pull up to my brownstone, the car that has been tailing me since I left Rachael's parks three spaces back.

"Fuck, you don't ask for much, do you? I'll see what I can do." He pauses. "Shit, I almost forgot why I called. You remember Fred from the local 79, right?"

"Sure," I reply, climbing the steps of my brownstone.

"I'm going to have you take the meeting with him today at 2:30. Unless you have other plans?"

"That won't be a problem, Pop. Hell, you'll be doing me a favor. You know how much I hate laundry." Looking out the narrow window to the left of my door, I don't see anyone get out of the red Honda. "I'm going to call Sebastian to drive me. I need him to keep a tail busy while I'm with Fred. Same place as usual?"

"A good horse never changes his stall, son. See you tonight."

Taking the stairs two at a time to my bedroom, I dial Sebastian.

"Yeah," his gruff voice comes over the line.

"Well, hello to you too, sunshine." I flop down on the

bed and cross my ankles. "You're sounding a little rough this morning."

"Went out drinking with Christian and Rafe last night. Don't tell those assholes they can drink me under the table now, or I'll never live it down. You sound downright chipper. It's freakin' creepy. You must have gotten laid last night."

His laugh makes me shake my head, that dick. I put my hand behind my head and lean into my pillows.

"You better pull it together in time to get me to a meeting at 2:30."

"What the fuck am I, Driving Miss Daisy?"

I hear him moving around, and water running in the background.

"They tailed me, leaving Rachael's apartment this morning. I need to slip into Finnegan's Bar undetected for a meeting with Fred. But . . . if you want me to call someone else to play cat and mouse with the FBI, I will."

"Get outta here, you know I live for that shit. Wait a second, do my ears deceive me? Did you say leaving her place this morning?"

"You heard me." Looking up at the ceiling, an image fills my mind of Rachael with her head thrown back, nails digging into my shoulders, screaming my name. "She'll be sharing her bed with me from now on."

Sebastian's Charger slides around the corner, the late afternoon sun momentarily blinding me. The car's back end is still straightening out as he switches lanes, sliding between two cars. He stays hidden between them for a few blocks before taking a tight left turn into the alley.

Unbuckling my seat belt, I reach for the door handle as he slows by the back door of the bar. In a well-practiced move, I open the car door while simultaneously stepping out onto the pavement and slamming the car door shut. Sebastian takes off down the alley as I walk in the bar's door.

The smell of fried food assails my nostrils. A large steel walk-in freezer takes up most of the space in the small hallway, with steel supply racks lining the other side. A tall gaunt kid washing dishes looks up as I pass him, but makes no motion to stop me. The kitchen is divided down the center of the room by a prep area. Walking along the left side of the kitchen, an obese man covered with acne takes a basket of fries out of the grease, turning his body sideways to let me pass.

The swinging door that leads from the kitchen to the bar area makes a whooshing noise as it swings closed behind me. Scanning the room, I see a set of restrooms to the right, followed by a long L-shaped bar. The head I'm looking for stands out halfway down the rows of booths on my left. Fred's fiery red hair and tall stature make him easy to pick out.

He inclines his head at me as I sit down across from him. Leaning back, I meet his direct gaze, waiting for him to finish sizing me up. His voice is deceptively mild, given his size.

"I admit to being a bit surprised when John said I'd be meeting with you instead."

"Why's that?"

"John's not that old to be turning over the reins already. How old are you, Vonni?"

"Twenty-seven, the same age you were when you became president of the construction union. You ran against the legendary old man McCready. Shocked the hell out of me when you won. Didn't think anyone could topple the old bird. As for Pop, he's still the head of the family. Think of me as . . . insurance. Should something happen to Pop, nothing changes for you."

"You know your history, I'll give you that." He looks around the bar before speaking again. "You saw the sign on Broadway and 215th Street?"

"I hear another high rise office building is going to be built at that location."

A nervous tick at the corner of his eye makes him blink rapidly. "Bids have been pouring in like crazy."

"Is that so?"

I got a bad feeling what came next wouldn't be the truth.

"The Lowest bid is 195 million."

He sits back, looking pleased with himself. For the moment, I let him think he got one over on me while I consider my next move. In moments like this, it occurs to me why Nonno insisted on playing both chess and poker with me as a kid.

"That's not what I hear from Will over in zoning."

I hadn't spoken to Will yet, but the look on Fred's face confirms my suspicions.

"Will doesn't have all the final numbers yet."

He seems downright pleased with his efforts to cover his tracks. Not so fast, junior.

"Not a problem." Watching a bead of sweat on his brow, I go in for the kill. "I'll phone him now."

Pulling out my phone from inside my suit jacket, I scroll through my contacts.

"Wait. Fuck. Forgive me, Vonni."

Still pretending to scan my contacts, I never look up from my phone. "What am I forgiving you for, Fred?"

"It was Vito's idea. I tell you a number too high, and he wins the bid."

"It's not his family's turn to win the bid though, is it, Fred?"

I shoot off a text to Sebastian that I'm five minutes out before I meet Fred's nervous gaze.

"No." He looks around again before he leans in. "Vito just got me killed, didn't he?"

"That depends on what you do now, Fred."

"Tell me, I'll do anything."

I understand his whiny tone, but it still grates on my nerves. He's been playing the game long enough to know better.

"Give me the real number." I lean in, lowering my voice. "Then you keep your fucking mouth shut."

EIGHT

RACHAEL

As I wait for Vonni to pick me up, Chantal's question about if I want more plagues me. The simple answer is, I don't know. In part, it depends on what Vonni wants. Since we are seeing each other today, I can rule out a one-night stand. If he's just looking for a casual Saturday night date, my answer is going to be no. The thought of him sleeping with me one night, and another girl the next, is unappealing. If he's looking for a serious relationship, then the answer is probably.

If I'm brutally honest with myself, the only reason for the probably is there's something about him that scares me. The physical attraction is obvious, but for me, I felt something much deeper last night. He makes me feel comfortable and confident in my skin. Like I can be the best version of myself.

Looking down at the green dress from my earlier shopping spree, I pick off a nonexistent fuzz from the skirt. Chantal assured me earlier that this dress would work no matter what Vonni's family had planned. The dress is at least comfortable, and I feel beautiful in it. A knock at the door makes me jump.

"You smell good," he says, burying his face in my neck and inhaling.

He kisses up the side of my neck, moving along my jaw before tasting my lips. His kiss is desperate and delicious. My hands run up his arms and around his neck, playing in the hair at his nape. He walks me backward into the apartment, running his hands down my back to my butt, grabbing it with both hands. With a groan, he breaks the kiss, taking a step back from me.

I point at the open collar of his pale pink dress shirt. "Every time we're together, you're wearing a suit, but no tie."

"I hate ties, they make me feel like I'm being choked." He runs his hands along my arms. "You're wearing my favorite color today."

"I'll have to remember that." I run my hand over his chest muscles. "Does this dress look ok? I don't want to show up underdressed."

"Cara, you look beautiful." His gaze travels from my face down to the leopard ballerina flats on my feet and back up. "Of course I like you better naked."

I grab my purse, trying to hide the pink in my cheeks. "Are you ready to go?"

His warm hand rests on the small of my back as he turns the lock, closing the door behind us.

Downstairs, I spot his SUV and head toward it. His long stride has him passing me before I can reach the door, and he pulls it open, helping me in.

"Where are we going?"

"My parents' house is outside the city. It will take us about forty-five minutes to get there."

He fishes his phone out from his coat pocket, plugging it in the dash. He looks down, scrolling through like he's driving and checking messages. I hear Snoop Dog's voice coming through the speakers, making me laugh, and eye him curiously.

"Do you like rap?" he asks, grabbing my hand.

"Yes, but I'm partial to the older stuff."

"I couldn't agree more."

On the drive we listen to his playlist, and I realize we have a lot of the same tastes in music. We leave the city behind, the houses becoming larger and more spread out. The streets are flawlessly manicured, and when we pull up to a guard shack, Vonni lowers his window to talk to a hulk of a man with a long goatee.

"Ben, how's the wife?"

"Still pregnant." He chuckles, his voice sounding just like Barry White's.

"Poor girl. What does that make, a week past her due date?"

"She's threatening to geld me if she goes another week."

Vonni makes a face as the wrought iron gates slide open. Trees line the long narrow driveway as we climb upward and, in the clearing, stands a large colonial-style house. The black shutters complement the white exterior, with columns on either side of a set of massive wooden doors.

A girl comes running out of the house, heading straight for the driver's side door as soon as we come to a stop. When Vonni gets out, she punches him in the arm.

"I had to hear about your date from Pop. Pop, for Christ's sake. You were supposed to call me with a full report."

"I've been a little busy. Besides, I'll do you one better. You get to be the first to meet her."

He grabs her hand, bringing her to where I'm standing by my door. As she comes closer, I can tell this is Vonni's twin sister. Her facial features are a carbon copy of Vonni's, only with a feminine edge. She's several inches shorter, and her build is more trim than muscular. A blue tank top is tucked into her short jean skirt. White Converse high tops look large on her dainty feet.

"You must be Rachael. I'm so excited to meet you, I'm Mandy."

"Tell me, was Vonni always this serious?" I ask with a devilish smirk on my face.

She giggles, leaving Vonni's side to put her arm through mine, leading me up to the house.

"You know, Vonni scares away all the men that are brave enough to bother coming around." Side by side, we walk through the front door. She drags me past a small foyer. "I've been waiting a very long time for payback."

A set of French doors lead to a massive screened-in porch where two men sit smoking cigars. They appear to be drinking some type of brown liquor as they talk. One of them looks to be in his seventies with a thick head of gray hair that in his youth was probably a very dark brown. Despite his advanced age, he has an air of danger about him. The other man is in his late forties or early fifties, with dark eyes and a thick head of salt and pepper hair. He's a head taller than the older man and broader with more muscle mass.

"Mandy, who do you have with you?" the older man asks. His voice holds all the smoothness of Vonni's, but with a distinctly Italian lilt to it.

Mandy bends forward to place a kiss on his cheek. "Nonno, this is Vonni's girl, Rachael."

"Aha, come closer, dear. I want to see the girl that's got my grandson all hot and bothered."

"Nonno, behave yourself," Vonni says from behind me as I extend my hand to shake the older man's warmly.

Nonno takes my hand in his, kissing the top of it. "What fun is that?"

I can't help but laugh. I'm pretty sure Nonno doesn't know what gets Vonni hot and bothered. He must be teasing Vonni about bringing me home with him. Word travels fast in this family if Nonno already knew about Vonni bringing me to dinner.

"He's too serious to be so young."

He has a mischievous twinkle in his eye that I find quite endearing. I'm betting he was quite the rascal in his day.

From behind me, Vonni clears his throat.

"Rachael, this is our Pop, John," Mandy says, pointing to the man with Nonno.

Nonno lets go of my hand so I can extend it to Vonni's dad. His handshake is warm and firm.

"Glad to have you here." John's voice is louder and rougher than either Nonno or Vonni's. His Brooklyn accent isn't as pronounced as Vonni's, and there's no trace of the Italian accent Nonno has. "You'll have to excuse Nonno. He never could behave himself around a pretty girl."

"Is this slander or were you a ladies' man?"

"Don't encourage him," John groans.

"I was a bit of a scoundrel before I met Vonni's grandmother." He glares at John before continuing. "Now that she's gone, I see no reason to be a monk. Johnny boy here would see me put out to pasture."

Mandy tries to smother a giggle behind her hand.

"Let's go meet the others before I have to fight Nonno for you," Vonni says, putting his hand on my side.

"Vonni, take her around, then come back to speak with Nonno and I for a minute."

Vonni nods at John, steering me toward the screen door with Mandy following behind. Outside, a group of women sit around a long glass-top table with an umbrella at each end for shade. Vonni's mother is obvious right away because both Vonni and Mandy are carbon copies of her.

"You must be Rachael." She stands, putting both her hands on my shoulders. "I'm Elena."

She brings me in close to envelop me in a hug. Waving Vonni off, she puts her arm around me, drawing me toward the table.

"These are my sister's. Tracy, Faye, Carrie, and Ashley. On the other side of the table are John's sisters. Carol and Jan. Ladies, this is Rachael."

The women stare at me before they all speak at once, drilling me with what feels like a million questions. Vonni lets out a long whistle, causing the ladies to quiet down and stare at him.

"Vonni, didn't your dad want to talk to you?" his mother asks, cutting him off before he can say anything to his aunts. "Go on, Rachael will be just fine with me."

Vonni backs away, mouthing "I'm sorry" before leaving me to the wolves.

"Now ladies." Elena claps her hands. "Let's not overwhelm the poor girl if we want her to come back."

All the women around the table nod their agreement and Elena turns to me.

"Do you like wine?"

"Now you're speaking my language," I tell her with a wide grin, grateful for the sweet buzz a glass would give me to loosen my nerves.

NINE

VONNI

Ma left me with no choice but to leave Rachael in her care. On the porch, Nonno moves over a seat so I can sit between them as Pop pours another shot of brandy. Leaning back in my chair, I hold out my hand and Nonno passes his cigar over to me. I take a long drag, filling my lungs to capacity, before handing it back. I'm not looking forward to telling Pop about our newest problem.

"How did your meeting go with Fred?" Pop asks, taking a drag of his cigar and blowing smoke out the side of his mouth.

"He sized me up, as expected." I drum my hand on my leg as I meet Pop's gaze. "Then he took me for a fool and gave me the wrong number. Apparently at Vito's urging."

"Cocksucker," Nonno bursts out. "Never trusted Vito as far as I could throw him."

Pop watches me as he inhales. "And what did you do about that?"

"Got the real number out of Fred, then told him to keep his mouth shut. I thought it might be helpful for Vito to think we lost the bid and we're none the wiser, for the time being, anyway. While Sebastian was playing keep away with the FBI, I called Will to verify all the bids."

"That's my boy," Nonno says, leaning over and clapping me on the back.

My brother Rafe walks onto the porch and sits down across from us. Pop pours another shot and slides it across the wicker glass-top table.

Rafe smirks. "You guys having a party without me?"

"More like a debriefing with cigars and brandy." Nonno smiles. "You're just in time. Here, have a puff off my cigar."

Rafe sits back, swirling his brandy and holding the cigar. He doesn't take a puff, instead he looks at me.

"Rachael came back squeaky clean."

"I didn't ask you to check Rachael out."

"No, you didn't, but I did," Pop says, meeting my gaze. "This is the first woman you've brought home, not just some girl you're fucking. Of course, I had Rafe check her out as a precaution." He raises his eyebrow at me before turning to Rafe. "Give us the particulars."

"Born and bred in a small town a few hours north of here. She was raised by her grandmother after her parents were killed by a drunk driver. Girl hasn't even gotten so much as a parking ticket in her life. Graduated from college with a three point nine GPA while working at a plastics plant full time. The only negative thing I could find out about her is that she's divorced. I figured nobody could be that clean, so I made some discreet inquiries. The only thing that turned up was apparently she's divorced because the prick couldn't keep it in his pants. She doesn't even have a single enemy, for fuck's sake."

As I listen to Rafe's report, I crack my knuckles. I understand why Pop did what he did, but it doesn't mean I have to like it, even though I'd have done the same thing in his position. In our world, we can't be too careful about the people we let into our lives. I should have seen this coming instead of being stupidly blindsided. My only consolation is at least my gut instinct about Rachael was right.

Rafe drinks his shot, then looks back and forth between Pop and me. "Interestingly enough, she has a tenuous connection to us."

"How so?" I ask him, crossing my arms.

His brow raises. "Kevin LaDeuc is her cousin."

An awkward silence fills the porch. Leaning forward, I put my elbows on my knees and look at Rafe.

"Since you already know her background, you might as well come meet her."

"I thought you'd never ask," Rafe says, letting out a breath.

Both of us rise and I put my hand on Pop's shoulder and gently squeeze before we head out. Rafe stops just outside the door and looks at the table that our family is currently congregating around. Frowning, he kicks a loose stone sitting on the cement.

"Are you mad at me?"

"No, Pop is not only your father, but your boss. You can't refuse an order from your boss. I'm not thrilled about it, but I don't hold it against either of you."

"Well then, lead the way," he says, his smirk back in place now that he knows we're ok.

TEN

RACHAEL

Deep into my fourth glass of wine, I look around the table. Elena's not hearing any of my attempts to cut myself off. Vonni's right, they are a little too much, but in my eyes that's what makes them so fantastic. Mandy sits next to me, supplying side information and answering questions in between drinking her margarita.

Tracy is an interior designer who lives in the city with her investment banker husband. Faye's a single writer who has colorful affairs with artists and was once asked to have sex on a canvas that later sold at auction. Carrie splits her time between the coasts to accommodate the schedule of her B list actor husband, Reggie Cray. Ashley works in the fashion district and has a long-term live-in boyfriend who works down at the docks. Jan is a hair stylist by trade, while Carol is a homemaker. Reading between the lines, I gather both Jan and Carol's husbands and their grown children work for John.

"How many of those have you had, Mandy?" A husky voice asks from behind us.

"Don't you have something better to do than monitor me, Seb?" Mandy looks at me, heaving a long-suffering sigh. "Rachael, this is Vonni's best friend, Sebastian. Seb, this is Vonni's girl, Rachael."

Turning around, I hold I out my hand. His hand's so large I can fit two of mine in one of his. I have to crane my neck to look up at his face. He's bald and clean shaven, with bulging muscles like a well-built man who spends lots of time in the gym and takes pride in his body.

"It's nice to put a face with a name," Sebastian says, giving me a smile, showing off a dimple in his left cheek.

I raise an eyebrow. "So Vonni's been talking about me?"

"I plead the fifth." He turns back to Mandy. "You didn't answer me."

"Unless you want me to grill you about anything he may have said about me." I go to poke him in the chest, except I'm sitting down, and a little tipsy, so I end up poking him in the stomach. "Leave Mandy to her margaritas."

Vonni walks up at that moment, followed by a younger guy with eyes the same shade as Vonni's. It looks totally different on him, however, because the blue of his eyes is a stark contrast to his dark hair and olive skin.

"Rachael, this is my younger brother Rafe," Vonni says, moving aside.

Instead of shaking my hand, he bends over it, placing a kiss on the back just like Nonno had done earlier. His deep blue eyes hold mine as he lingers over my hand. Looking up at him, I notice Rafe has John's denser muscle mass and taller height.

"Let my girl's hand go before you lose yours," Vonni says.

"Took him long enough to say something." Rafe drops my hand, giving Vonni a shit-eating grin. "Must be losing my touch."

Mandy hiccups, causing me to break out in raucous laughter.

"You better check your girl," Sebastian tells Vonni,

shaking his head.

Vonni smirks. "She's talking shit to you, is she?"

"She's gotten your sister drunk," Sebastian says, cocking an eyebrow.

"I'm pretty sure it was all my aunts that got them both drunk."

"The aunts have definitely been getting them drunk," Rafe says, eyeing Vonni.

"He's messing with Mandy and ruining our buzz with his judgment." I look up at him and smile. "Still like you anyway though, Sebastian."

Mandy's head bobs up and down in confirmation.

"What's going on here?" Christian asks, joining the already full party.

Sebastian crosses his arms over his massive chest. "Vonni's girl is a bad influence on Mandy."

"Get the fuck out of here." Christian laughs. "You think everyone is a bad influence on Mandy if she looks like she's having any fun."

"Take a fucking walk, Christian."

"Can you believe this fucking guy?" Christian asks me, shrugging.

"Mandy and I have a few drinks and Sebastian's all uptight about it. Oh well, maybe we should give him a break on being a party pooper as long as he drinks with us."

"Oh, shit." Christian pulls out a chair and motions to the guy standing beside him. "Rachael, this is Vonni's younger brother Luke."

Luke is a younger version of Vonni, except for his darker brown eyes. He inclines his head and looks between Mandy and me before saying, "I'm going to see what's keeping dinner, I have a feeling we'll need to get some food in them before things get ugly."

At the other end of the table, Vonni's aunts are still drinking and chatting. Sebastian disappears into the house, coming out a few minutes later with a handful of beers.

He gives me a salute as he says, "If you can't beat her, join her."

"I appreciate you coming over to the dark side."

"It'll take a miracle to get the stick out of Seb's butt," Mandy says, sticking out her tongue at him.

"A girl who can quote Star Wars and likes nineties rap? I think I just fell in love," Vonni says before walking off to join the guy's conversation.

Once Vonni is out of earshot, I ask Mandy, "How long has Sebastian had a thing for you?"

Taking a sip of her margarita, Mandy starts coughing and sputtering. Patting her on the back, I wave off Vonni's look of concern.

"What makes you say that? Sebastian and I have known each other since we were kids and never dated."

"Let me guess, he's overprotective in the extreme. When you bring a guy around, he acts like an asshole? Plus, I've caught him eye fucking you about three different times."

"He'll never make a move," she whispers, peeking over at him. "He's my brother's best friend, and he works for my father."

"How do you feel about him?"

I give her a long look, daring her with my eyes to deny what I already know.

"I've been in love with him since I was fifteen," she huffs, blowing out a breath so hard it ruffles the piece of hair hanging in her face. "Wow, I've never admitted that out loud before."

She leans over to hug me as Luke comes out of the house, followed by several people carrying trays of food. Elena fills up my wine, even though I shake my head no. Vonni will have to carry me to the car if I don't sip lightly during dinner. The flavor of the chicken piccata explodes in my mouth, eliciting a moan that comes out louder than I intend.

"I think this is the first time I've ever been jealous of food," Vonni whispers in my ear, discreetly adjusting himself under the table.

The laugh that bubbles up out of me at his predicament has everyone turning to stare before they resume their own conversations. Looking around the table as I eat, I can't keep the smile off my face. Laughter and merriment are everywhere I look.

"It's getting late, are you ready to head back?" Vonni asks, as the servers come back to clean up.

"Let me say goodbye to everyone."

He smirks. "That will take another hour."

On the way out, Nonno's the last one I come to.

"Tell Vonni to take you to Nonno's place one night for dinner," he whispers in my ear, before Vonni grabs me and pushes me toward the door.

Helping me into the car in typical Vonni fashion, he shamelessly grabs me to assist. He climbs in, starting down the drive, and the gate opens automatically for us to drive through, Vonni giving Ben a wave as we pass.

He watches me out of the corner of his eye. "You and Mandy seemed to hit it off."

"We did." I lay my head against the headrest of the seat. "It's nice to have a girl my age to have fun with. I like her."

He runs his fingers along my hand while he drives, always having to move his fingers. My lids grow heavy as I look out the window at the streetlights flying past.

Light coming on inside the car wakes me and Vonni is standing at my door, ready to help me onto the sidewalk. He winds his hand around my hip, leading me up the front steps as I hopelessly sway to one side. His thigh brushes against mine as he helps me up the three flights to my apartment. After digging around in my purse for the keys, he let us in.

"Vonni."

I lean heavily against him as we walk side by side down the hallway toward my bedroom.

"Hmm, cara?"

He moves sideways, walking us through the doorway into

my bedroom before gently laying me down on the bed.

"I had a wonderful time meeting your family," I murmur, curling into my pillow and shutting my eyes.

ELEVEN

RACHAEL

The alarm wakes me up and as I turn it off, I hear a groan beside me. Vonni lies on his stomach, naked from the waist up.

He turns onto his side, wiping a hand down his face. "What time is it?"

"Seven." I lift the covers and look down at myself. "Vonni, I'm still wearing my clothes from yesterday."

"Yeah, you took your shoes off and fell into bed." He puts his arm around me, drawing me closer. "Last night I plugged in your phone for you before I crawled into bed."

"Thank you." Toying with the comforter, I ask, "Did I do anything embarrassing yesterday? Your mom kept pouring wine, and I can't handle more than two glasses."

"Embarrassing, no." He gives me a lopsided grin. "However, I found your talking shit to Sebastian hilarious."

"He doesn't hate me, does he?"

"He finds you interesting," Vonni says, leaning on his elbow. "No one is brave enough to give him back what he dishes out."

"Brave enough or stupid enough?" I try to move his arm. "Vonni, I have to get ready for work."

"Damn, are you sure?" he asks, kissing along my neck.

"Vonni." I push against his chest with the flat of my hand. "Not that I don't love where this is going, but I can't be late on my first day. We'll have to continue this later."

With a long-suffering sigh, he releases me, and on my way to the shower I hear his phone ringing. A case of nerves is settling in the pit of my stomach, and I stand under the hot spray with my eyes closed, trying to psych myself up for the day ahead. The sound of a knock on the shower door has me blinking water from my eyelashes.

"There's a problem I have to take care of this morning." He leans against the door, raising his voice to be heard over the spray of the shower. "I'm heading out to meet Christian."

I wipe my palm across the glass so I can see him through the steam. "Is everything all right?"

"Yeah. It's nothing I can't handle." He looks up and down my wet, naked body before heaving a sigh. "Fuck. I'd rather be in the shower with you."

He shakes his head and leaves the bathroom.

For my first day, I choose the blue pencil skirt outfit from my shopping expedition with Chantal, and as I sit at the breakfast bar drinking coffee, I feel pretty good about myself. From beside me, my phone dings and I see a message.

CHANTAL: Are you up?

ME: I'm getting ready to go to work.

A minute later he comes breezing through the kitchen, pouring himself a cup of coffee. I'm going to have to stock up on coffee with my bestie popping over whenever he feels like it.

"Would you like to watch my show tonight? I figure I'd better ask before that handsome man gets to you."

"I'd love to come to your show. I've never been to one, and it sounds fun."

"I'll bring back your cup when I pick you up at eight," he says, giving me a quick hug before he heads out the door.

With a last sip of coffee, I grab my purse and head out the door myself. Before I pull out into traffic, I type in the address for the docks into my car's GPS. Nineties hip-hop on Sirius Radio fills the car and I zone out on the drive. As I approach the docks, I turn the radio down, but it doesn't take long for me to figure out where to go. My cousin Kevin was right, it looks like a warehouse that has been converted into offices.

Parking, I head toward what I'm hoping is the front door. A security guard sits at a large desk right by the elevators.

"What can I do you for?" he asks, hitching his pants up over his round stomach.

He rubs his hand across his handlebar mustache, waiting for an answer. It's doubtful he can run anyone down, but I have to give him credit for making me squirm.

"I'm hoping you can tell me where to find Kendra Meehan." I give him my most radiant smile, while I read his name from the tag hanging off his navy button-down shirt. "Today's my first day, Sam."

"Top floor. When you get off the elevator, go to the left. She's the last office at the end." His face softens. "Got an excellent view of the docks from up there."

"I appreciate it. I'm low on the totem pole, so I'll have a windowless cube. It will be nice to take breaks and look out at the water, though. See you around, Sam."

He's right, the view of the harbor is spectacular. Trying not to get lost in the view too long, I continue down the hall. When I reach the office he said was Kendra's, I knock before popping my head in the door.

She looks up at me, throwing her long dark ponytail over one shoulder, as she stands up to greet me, and I try to keep my mouth from hanging open. Her olive skin is as flawless as her figure.

"I'm Rachael LaDeuc." I walk forward and extend my hand. "You must be Kendra Meehan. I'm excited to be working for you. Kevin gave glowing reviews about how you and your dad run the place."

"Kevin and Dad were always fond of one another." She gives me a quick once over. "There's no mistaking the family resemblance."

"The LaDeuc clan all look alike, I'm afraid."

"That's not a bad thing. I dated the handsome devil for a year. How is Kevin doing?"

"Much the same as you remember, I'm sure. Thank you for asking."

She nods her head toward the chair in front of her desk before sitting back down, her lip curling in a small half smile. "I must admit, when I heard from him after so long, it intrigued me. When he told me what a paragon you are, I had to snatch you up. He may be many things, but a liar was never one."

"The LaDeuc's are honest to a fault, and hard workers. I'm sure you remembered that, otherwise you wouldn't be giving me a chance."

"I understand he went to work for the plastics plant in your hometown."

"Most of the LaDeucs have worked there at some point. I've held several positions over the years. My most recent position was in Human Resources."

"I believe Kevin's exact word to describe you was brainiac. I can use a girl like you. If you're anything like him, you'll be easy to get along with. That's a bonus since I'm known for being difficult to work with. Let's get you settled in."

I follow her through an adjoining door into a small office right before hers. Filing cabinets line the wall opposite the oak L-shaped desk.

"This will be your office. I put your log-in on a sticky near your computer. You'll also find a folder with all the new hire paperwork to help get you started. Come find me after you settle in. There's a supply closet one door down. If there's something you need that's not there, make a list."

Over the next half hour, I settle in and play around in some programs, jotting down a list of questions. Notebook in hand, I head to Kendra's office. When I knock on the adjoining door, she looks up, motioning for me to come in.

"Bring your chair around next to me so you can see my screen. I'll show you how everything works."

I bring a chair around to her side of the desk, but as soon as I sit down, there's a kick at the door. When I look up, I see Vonni standing there. My mouth falls open, and his confident stride falters for a second.

"Rachael, what are you doing here?"

"This is my new job. I'll be working for Kendra."

Kendra's eyes go between the two of us. "You know Rachael?"

"We met at a diner on Friday night."

His explanation baffles me, leaving me to wonder what I am to him. To everyone else, I'm with him or referred to as Vonni's girl. Today, however, he tells my very attractive female boss that we just met at a diner. Granted, that's true, but it still pisses me off. Rubbing the back of his neck, he looks back and forth between Kendra and me.

"Rachael, why don't you wait for me in your office. The business Mr. Moran has with the company is . . . sensitive."

Grabbing my notepad, I hustle through the adjoining door before quietly closing it behind me. At my desk I log back in, becoming absorbed with learning the new programs. A shadow falls across my computer screen. Looking up, I see Christian smiling down at me.

"What are you doing here?" he asks, sitting down and making himself comfortable in my office.

"I'm working for Kendra." I lean back in my chair. "Today's my first day."

"Dragon Lady, best of luck to you." He whistles low. "They all quit within a few months."

"She mentioned she's going to appreciate me being easy to work with because she's not. Still, she can't be that bad. My cousin dated her for a year."

"No shit. What's your cousin's name?"

"Kevin LaDeuc."

"I know that kid. He worked on the docks until about a year ago. Real easygoing, didn't fuck with anybody. Everybody was sad to see him go. Now I'm looking at you, I can see the resemblance in both looks and personality. How is he, anyway?"

"Same old. Work during the day, and party at night. I wish he'd settle down with a nice girl. He's politely told me to butt out every time I try to introduce him to a girl."

"He went out drinking with me and my friends a few times. Never took a girl home. Makes sense now I know he was hitting Dragon Lady."

Christian has a way of being blunt that I admire.

I try to fake a nonchalant attitude as I ask, "Did Vonni go out with you guys?"

"You've got to be shitting me. Vonni doesn't go out drinking. He knew Kevin from here, but that's it."

"He never drinks, or goes out?"

"Not usually. I mean he'll have a beer, glass of wine, or an occasional shot here or there. I've never seen him drunk. He's too controlled for that. He also can't dance for shit."

Sensing a shift in atmosphere, I look up. Vonni's leaning against the doorjamb, his stormy expression causing the laughter to die on my lips.

TWELVE

VONNI

My dream of keeping Rachael from ever finding out about my family disappears along with her. She closes the adjoining door behind her with a resounding click. The best I can hope for now is to protect her from the harsh realities of my world. There's no way Kendra won't tell her who I am or what my family does. After all, Kendra blames me for Kevin leaving her. Of course, it can't have anything to do with the fact that even on a good day everyone thinks she's a bitch.

"To what do I owe the pleasure?"

Sarcasm drips from her voice as I sit down across from her.

"Leo will roll up to the docks tonight in a 1967 Shelby Mustang GT500. I've already given him the container number where he's parking it. I need you to make sure everything goes smoothly."

She crosses her arms and gives me a hard stare, her bitch persona on full display. "Going to our friends in the Middle East?"

"Yes." I lean back in the chair, watching her. "I don't need to remind you about our agreement, or your considerable compensation."

"I know my place. If there's nothing else, I have a new employee to train."

"About that." Standing, I put both my hands on her desk. "You will not give Rachael a hard time because of her association with me."

"What is your association with her?"

"Watch yourself, Kendra," I growl as I lean in. "It's no concern of yours, her association with me, but leave her out of our dealings or I'll make that compensation dwindle."

Turning, I walk out of her office without another word. My nerves being on edge after dealing with Kendra is nothing new. She's one of the most trying women I have ever had the misfortune to meet. Christian's voice, followed by Rachael's laughter, fills the hallway, infuriating me further.

Leaning against the doorjamb, I take Rachael in. Damn, she looks beautiful when she laughs. My hands ball into fists. I want to be the one to make her laugh. She looks up, her laughter dying when she sees me standing there.

"Look who I found," Christian says, swiveling in his chair to look at me.

"I see. You ready to go? We have some other stops to make."

He stands, smiling at Rachael. "See ya later, doll."

"Kendra is ready for you now." My tone comes out more clipped than I intend because of my desire to punch Christian in the face. Softening, I tell her, "I'll call you later."

"What's got your panties in a twist?" Christian asks as we leave Rachael's office.

"Nothing." I push the first-floor button on the elevator. "I need to talk to Pete before we head out. Meet me at the car."

"Whatever you say, dude."

Christian steps off the elevator, heading toward the car with his usual slow swagger.

With a wave at the security guard on my way past, I open the door, turning toward the docks. Walking with my hands in my pockets, I look for Pete. In a sea of navy hats, at first, he's hard to spot, but I see him off to the side, having a smoke with two other guys. I nod my head toward the guys, partially as a greeting and partially as a way of telling them to leave us; they split off, leaving Pete to turn toward me. His grin's warm as he waits for me to get close.

"I was wondering what made those two take off in such a hurry." He reaches out to shake my hand. "Ashley told me you brought a girl to dinner."

"Wouldn't you know it? I show up here on business, and there she is in Kendra's office."

Pete takes another cigarette out of his pocket, offering it to me. When I shake my head, he puts it between his lips and lights it.

"No shit." He flicks the ash off to the side. "Your girl is Kendra's new assistant?"

"So it would seem."

"Damn, she might regret that decision after a few weeks. None of those poor girls last long."

"I had a talk with Kendra, but I don't trust her not to take her anger with me out on Rachael. I need you to keep an eye on my girl for me. Make sure nobody bothers her."

"You got it." Pete throws his cigarette down, grinding it under his work boot. "I'll call you if I run into any trouble."

"I owe you one. You coming next Sunday to dinner?"

"Shit, and face all those squawking broads?" He walks away, turning around long enough to say, "No, thanks."

With my hands in my pockets, I walk toward the car, laughing and shaking my head.

THIRTEEN

RACHAEL

With a sigh, I go back into Kendra's office. She looks at me out of the corner of her eye when I sit down next to her.

"I don't involve myself in my employees' personal lives, but Kevin adores you, so I'm going to make an exception this once. Take my advice and stay away from the Morans."

She turns back to her computer, acting as if she hasn't just dropped a bombshell on me as she carries on with training. Something's not right, but I can't grill my new boss on my first day.

The rest of the morning goes by in a blur, and before I know it, Kendra's sending me to lunch. Since I didn't bother to bring anything on my first day, I ask Kendra what's close by. Of all the places she listed, the French cafe intrigued me the most.

My hands drum on the wrought iron table as I stare out the window. My brain is going a mile a minute, and it's not processing anything I'm seeing. I order tomato bisque soup and macaroni salad, a strange combination, but my taste buds seem to be happy, and my brain has had time to catch up to the whirring sensations I've had all morning since Vonni left my office.

I can't help but feel something's up with him. He acted strange from the moment he saw me in Kendra's office. With no more time to devote to figuring it out, I head out the doors and back to my new job.

In the elevator, I try to forget about Vonni's change in behavior and focus on work. Before long, I hear a knock on my door, and I assume the man standing in the doorway is a dockworker because he's wearing a royal blue shirt with the company's emblem. If I had to guess, I'd put him in his midforties or early fifties. Even with the blue cap on his head, I can tell he has a thick head of dark hair. His muscular physique and hazel eyes against the tan of his skin make for an overall eye-catching combination.

"Can I help you?" I ask, pointing at the chair in front of my desk.

"I think you met my girl yesterday, Ashley Demaris." He takes off his hat before sitting down. "She's Vonni's aunt on his Ma's side."

"Yes, I did. We had a fantastic time together. You're a very lucky man." I try to recall if Ashley ever mentioned him by name, but I'm coming up short. "I'm afraid I don't know your name, though."

"Pete Ferreira," he says, extending his hand across the desk.

"Pleased to meet you, Pete. How did you know to come look for me up here?"

"Vonni came and got me. He asked me to spread the word about who you were, and to keep an eye out for you. If you need anything at all, or anyone bothers you, let me know."

Vonni has some gall to tell my boss we met at a diner yet sends Ashley's other half to scare off the poor dock workers. None of which would ever be likely to say two words to me. Then something he said sinks in and bothers me.

"Pete, who am I?"

He shifts in his chair. "Vonni's girl."

"Why would the guys on the dock care who I date?"

"Well, they wouldn't if he was just some guy." He gives me a beseeching look. "He ain't though, he's a Moran."

"Pete, I'm new to the area, and I don't know what that means."

"The Morans run this city along with five other families." He's crestfallen at the blank look on my face. "He didn't tell you anything, did he?"

"Evidently not, so spill it, Pete."

"I don't think I should." He sits up straighter in his chair. "Maybe you should talk to Vonni."

He stands up, but I'm not about to let him go until I have answers. Coming around my desk, I stand in front of him with my arms crossed.

"I know his family is powerful, or rich, or both. You told me they run the city, but I don't quite understand what that means. Run the city, how? I'll never tell a soul that I heard it from your lips. I just want to know what I'm getting myself into."

He pushes past me to shut my office door. "I won't tell you outright, because it's not my place to do that, but I will tell you this. Run is the wrong word to use."

He looks around as if something in my office will give him the right description.

"Are you suggesting the Morans are in the Mafia?"

He says nothing, but the stoic look on his face had me wondering if I was right, or at least in the ballpark.

"I came to say hello and tell you if you need anything, all you have to do is ask. I've been here a long time and know my way around."

His words don't register as all the pieces fall into place in my brain.

"You ok?" he asks, his voice full of concern.

"I'll be fine," I lie as I inhale softly, but I'm not able to keep my thoughts inside. "How could I be so blind to not see this! Vonni's sudden change in behavior today makes perfect sense."

Pete turns toward the door, leaving me to my rambling before he gives me a look over his shoulder. "Again, anything at all, I mean anything, you come get me. If you don't see me, ask one of the guys to fetch me."

"Thanks, Pete. I worked for a plastics plant for a long time before I came here, I know how to handle myself."

With a curt bob of his head, he leaves my office. Pulling myself together, I head for Kendra's office for the rest of my training. It's going to be a very long afternoon.

FOURTEEN

VONNI

My call goes to voice mail, making me grit my teeth. Christian comes out of the convenience store across the street, shoving a wad of bills into his suit jacket. He slides into the SUV beside me, shaking his head at my dark scowl.

"What's wrong with you now?"

"Rachael's not answering her phone."

I glare down at it, like it's the phone's fault.

"Is she still at work?"

"How the hell would I know that?" I look at my watch. "It's five thirty, she should be home by now."

"Hand me the phone before you drive me fucking nuts today."

Holding out his hand, he wiggles his fingers in my direction until I give him my phone. I lean over, watching him install an application on it. Once it's downloaded, he imports Rachael's contact information into it and a map pops up with a white dot on it. When he zooms in with his fingers, I recognize the street names around Rachael's apartment.

"She's fine, she's at home," he says, handing me back my phone.

"I think she discovered who I am today, and that's why she's not answering her phone. She's running now she knows what my name means."

"Don't let her run then." He takes his phone out of his pocket as he pulls out into traffic. "I'm calling Rafe. I can't deal with your cranky ass sober."

Looking down at my phone, I watch Rachael's dot. Still at home.

ME: Call me.

"What's up?" Rafe's voice fills the car over Bluetooth.

"Vonni's being a pain in my ass today. This broad has him tied up in knots. All because he thinks she figured out who he is. Now he don't know if he's coming or going."

"My girl is none of your concern."

"You didn't think you could keep her in the dark, did you? Half the fucking city knows who you are. The other half that don't, are at least wise enough to recognize our last name."

Rafe's trying to be logical, I don't want logical. I want to punch something.

Still no response, and the dot hasn't moved.

ME: We need to talk.

"See what I'm dealing with. No fucking answer because the answer is he thought he could keep shit under wraps. You ask me it's better she finds out early on and learns to deal with it. I mean it's not like she's off fucking some dude, she's at home for Christ's sake."

My murderous glare at the mere mention of Rachael fucking another dude shuts Christian up.

"Shit, always running your damn mouth, Christian," Rafe says, diffusing a situation that he can tell is about to turn ugly. "Meet me over at Jefferson's Pub. Try not to get yourself shot before Luke and I can get there."

Silence hangs heavy in the car and looking down at my phone again I see the dot still hasn't moved. Rachael still hasn't responded either. Never in my life have I chased after a woman. Christian's right, she has me tied up in knots.

"Fuck," I yell, throwing my phone at the floorboard of the car.

With my head against the back of the seat, I close my eyes. My phone dings from the floor. Still, I sit there, afraid to look at my phone. What if the message says fuck off?

"If you don't read that damn message, I'm wrecking this car."

The asshole is just crazy enough to do it, so I pick up my phone and look down at the display.

"Don't hold out on me now after I've dealt with your bullshit all day."

"She says she's going to Chantal's show tonight."

He pulls into the back parking lot of the bar. "Show, what kind of show?"

Distracted, I get out of the car. "Drag show."

"Well, that's not a bad thing, right?" He meets me around the front of the SUV, falling in step as we walk up the alley. "I mean, how much trouble can she get into at a drag show? Let her blow off some steam. Come to terms with how shit is. Dude, give her some space."

At the mouth of the alley, I stand, scanning the street. Christian turns to the left, and after another quick look, I follow. He holds the heavy oak door open for me to precede him.

As I step into the gloom, my eyes do a quick scan of hands. Not sensing anything out of place, I head toward the bar that runs along the entire left side of the place. Twinkle lights hang along the top portion of the mirror behind the bar. My hip rests against the edge of the wooden-top bar as I glance into the mirror, surveying the booths behind me.

"What can I get ya, laddie?"

"Two beers." The bartender reaches under the bar and pulls out two bottles, cracking the tops open before he hands them to me. With a nod, I hand him two twenties. "Keep the change."

He smiles, his dimples pronounced in his round face. "I'll send ye another round, then."

Grabbing the beers, I turn toward the booth that Christian occupies. I slide in across from him, handing him his beer. Midway through my first sip, I see Sebastian walking in. Raising my beer in salute, I signal him. With a nod, he walks along the row of booths.

I slide over to make room for him. "Rafe, call you?"

"We were doing some collections when Christian called. Rafe will be in once he gets off the phone." He gives me a sideways look. "Heard the entire conversation."

"Great." I toy with my beer bottle, peeling the label. "Going to give me shit too?"

He looks at the front door, motioning to Rafe and Luke with his hand. "Nope."

Christian slides over for Rafe, while Luke takes a bar stool sitting at the head of the table.

"Sorry guys, I can't stay long." Rafe smirks. "Danika called."

"Is that the chick with the hot sister?" Christian asks.

"Hot cousin, but yes." Rafe cuts a glance at Christian. "It took a lot of smooth talking to get back into her good graces. You fucked her cousin and never called her back."

Luke snorts. "Tell us something new."

"Hey, I was upfront with the girl." Christian looks around at us. "Every girl in this city knows, I don't do girlfriends." He nods in my direction. "This poor fucker here is why."

Luke laughs. "You don't do girlfriends 'cause no girl will put up with your shit."

"That is beside the point," Christian says, causing everyone to break out in laughter.

Rafe looks down at his phone. "Shit, that's my cue, guys."

Luke slides into his spot, signaling the bartender for a fresh round of beers. He looks down at his phone before meeting my eyes.

"Don't tell me you have a hot date too?"

"No." He rolls his eyes at me. "More like recon."

"Pop has you watching someone?"

I find this puzzling because Pop tells me most things.

"It's not for Pop." He watches me for a second. "I told my girl not to go to a party tonight. I'm tracking her to make sure she listens."

"Really." Leaning in, I give him a sideways glance. "Since when did you get a girl?"

"See, this is why I don't say shit, everyone is so nosy."

"You mean like how the entire family is involved in my love life?"

"Fine. It's complicated." He lowers his voice. "She won't turn eighteen for another three months." As he looks down at his phone again, his ears turn red. That's always his telltale sign that he's pissed. "I gotta go. She didn't fucking listen."

He slides out of the booth and stalks off toward the door.

"Hold up, Luke, I'm coming," Christian calls after him. Smiling at us, he winks. "I feel like this shit is too good to pass up."

Sebastian takes a swig of his beer. "Twenty bucks says Luke pulls a gun on Christian by the end of the night."

With a sigh, I shake my head. Luke's grown and I have my own problems to contend with. Something Christian had said earlier and seeing Luke chase after his girl gives me an idea. No way am I letting my girl run from me.

"Seb, drop me off at Rachael's apartment."

FIFTEEN

RACHAEL

When I enter my apartment, I feel both dejected and tired. Work seems to be a success. Kendra isn't as terrible as Christian led me to believe, at least not yet, and she appears to be satisfied with me. Throwing my purse down, I head straight for my wine collection, kicking off my shoes as I go.

My purse begins to buzz and sing as I pour myself a glass. After finally locating my phone, the caller ID confirms what I suspected, it's Vonni. There's no way I'm talking to him right now. He can leave a message.

Wine in hand, I leave my apartment and head for Chantal's. If he can walk into my place, I can walk into his. As I reach for the door handle, a stranger opens the door and stands there, leaving me looking around, confused.

"Sorry, I'm looking for Chantal."

"You got the right place, come in." He steps aside to let me in, shutting the door behind us. "C, a little dark-haired girl is here looking for you."

He peeks around the door casing in the kitchen. "Hey girl,

hey."

"Bestie, I need to talk to you."

"Girl, sit down. Make yourself comfy, I'll be back after I deal with this diva. By the way, this is my cousin DeShawn."

Looking over at DeShawn, I realize they have the same flawless skin and figure. The only exception being that DeShawn is tall.

"Pleased to meet you, DeShawn," I say, shaking his hand.

"What's a cute girl like you doing hanging out with him?" He sits, motioning toward the kitchen.

"He's good people. Besides, you're here."

"I'm related to his ass." He raises a dark brow as he leans back. "Tell me, you got a boyfriend?"

Chantal comes and sits next to me on the caramel-colored love seat with a matching glass of wine.

"Cheers, bitch." We clink our glasses, and then he looks over at DeShawn. "She got a cute man. Leave my girl alone."

"I'm not sure what I have or don't have anymore."

Chantal leans in and pats my leg. "Tell me all about it."

"Wait for me, I'm going to get my drink," DeShawn says over his shoulder as he goes into the kitchen. "I love juicy drama."

With a snort, I wait for him to return. He sits down with a shot glass and a fifth of Hennessy.

He rolls his hand in my direction, digging out a cigar and lighting it. "Continue."

"Do you mind if I have a shot of that and a puff of your cigar?" I ask him, deciding I need more than wine tonight.

"You are going to smoke and drink Hennessy with me?" At my nod, he laughs. "Well, shit."

He gets up again, returning with another glass. Before he pours, he hands me the cigar.

"I love Hennessy." I knock back a full shot, taking a long drag off his cigar. "Do you know you can mix it with sweet tea?"

Both men sit there staring at me.

"Now if you tell me you make fried chicken, I'm going to get with you, man or no man," DeShawn says, leaning toward me.

"I make fried chicken, but wait until I go to the store again. I threw out the hot sauce I had when I moved."

He stands and holds out his hand. "That's it bitch, come on, we're going to your place."

"Sit your ass back down and quit messing with her," Chantal says, with a sideways look at DeShawn.

"You're right, I better hear her story first. See if she's crazy. I can't have another damn crazy woman on my hands."

"I think I might be a little too crazy for you." I hand him back his cigar. "Chantal, I wish I had saved myself some trouble and told you Vonni's last name. His name is Giovanni Moran."

"Yup, your ass is crazy." DeShawn lets out a low whistle. "I'm not ending up sleeping with the fish."

"Yeah, that's why I'm mixing wine and liquor tonight."

Chantal holds a hand to his chest, a look of utter shock passing across his face. "There's no way you could have known, you're not from here. I know his name, of course, but not what he looks like, or I would have told you. How did you find out?"

"Vonni was down at the docks for a meeting with my boss." I look down, toying with my empty glass. "His aunt's boyfriend came to my office. He told me Vonni asked him to keep an eye out for me. When I asked why Vonni would do that, he gave me enough clues for me to figure it out. I don't know why I didn't see it before."

"Well, there are perks to being Giovanni Moran's girlfriend. You can do worse." He nods his head toward DeShawn. "Much worse."

"Hey, you supposed to be my family," DeShawn says, catching on.

Chantal shrugs. "I just calls 'em as I see 'em."

"Chantal, what am I going to do? I have feelings for him.

I know that sounds crazy because I have only known him for such a short time, but when I am with him, it feels right. He has this way about him that makes all my insecurities disappear. I've never had a connection like this with any other guy before, not even my ex-husband."

"Here's what you're going to do." He wags his finger at me. "You're going to knock back another shot. Go home and put on something slutty. We're going to dinner, then my show. After the show, you'll go home and go to bed. If you still want Vonni in the morning, you'll deal with whatever problems arise as they come."

DeShawn hands me another shot, which I throw back before standing to do what Chantal said to do.

"I'll be right back."

In front of my closet, I stand there buzzed, debating on what I'm going to wear. Chantal walks into my bedroom, with DeShawn following on his heels. Chantal pushes me out of the way, rummaging through my closet. He hems and haws, moving on to my drawers. Chantal holds up a white corset.

"Yeah, that one is sexy." DeShawn nods.

Chantal goes back into the closet, pulling out a black and white plaid schoolgirl style skirt.

"Fella's, I'm not Britney Spears."

DeShawn laughs. "You right, she has a small ass."

"Just hand me whatever you want me to wear, Chantal."

In the bathroom I stare into the mirror, and I must admit it's slutty and not half bad. There's a knock on the door.

"Come in."

Chantal hands me multiple strings of pearls in varying sizes. "Put this on."

"Put these on girl," DeShawn says, holding up a pair of black stilettos.

After I put everything on, I stand in front of the boys for inspection. They shake hands with matching looks of satisfaction on their faces.

"Let's go, boys."

"I have to drop by my apartment real quick to pick up my bag for the show," Chantal says, leaving my bedroom.

While I'm waiting for Chantal out in the hall, I look down at my phone, seeing two texts from Vonni. My go-to move when I need to get out of my head is avoidance, but I decide to send him a reply.

ME: I'm going to Chantal's show tonight.

Then I turn off my phone before taking Chantal's hand as we walk down three flights of stairs. I need him to keep me steady since I'm tipsy and wearing my big girl shoes. From the back seat of Chantal's car, I look out the window as he drives. Their jokes and banter keep my mind occupied and off Vonni Moran for a while.

We pull up to a seedy-looking dive bar for dinner. Just inside the door, a life-size Charlie Chaplin statue is standing there to greet you. Old, framed Hollywood premiere posters hang on the walls and there's a basketball game playing by our booth. DeShawn and I watch that, while Chantal sits on the other side, people watching as we split an array of munchies.

"We have to go soon, C." DeShawn looks at his watch. "You'll need time to get ready before the show."

I take a last sip of my Coke. "Are you coming for the show too, DeShawn?"

"Shit, I have nothing else to do," he says with a shrug as he holds the door open for me.

Chantal's club is around the corner from the bar, so it only takes us a minute to get there. Chantal has a special parking pass that allows us to pull into an alleyway to the right of a row of townhomes. Each one is a separate club with interconnecting interiors, and Chantal takes us through the center door.

"I'm going to get a good seat," I tell the boys, weaving my way through the maze of small round tables toward the stage positioned at the center of the room.

DeShawn pulls out a chair next to me, so we can both see the stage. As soon as we sit down, a heavily muscled man wearing only a speedo and a bow tie shows up asking if we want drinks. Ordering a glass of wine, I look around, watching as the club fills up.

To pass the time before the show starts, DeShawn and I people watch until everything goes black, and a spotlight illuminates the announcer, who also doubles as comic relief for the night.

Chantal takes the stage wearing a sleeveless, red sequin floor-length gown with a crisscross design in the back. His heels sparkle in the light reflecting off his ruby necklace. He's a handsome man, but he's nothing less than stunning as a woman. The crowd goes wild as he sings "I'm Every Woman," and I'm transfixed as I stare up at him.

At the end of the song, he walks off the stage. He moves through the crowd, flirting at every table. When he reaches us, he rubs his gloved hand along my back, giving me a wink as he heads backstage.

There are a few more acts before he takes the stage again. All of them hold me in their thrall, but none quite like Chantal. This time he takes the stage wearing a silver backless cocktail dress. As he sings "Born This Way," the entire crowd stands up singing along with him. He cups his ear, showing the crowd that we should sing louder. I jump up and down and scream along to the song until I grow hoarse.

When he makes the rounds again, everyone rushes to talk to him. A swelling in my chest overwhelms me as I watch him. The crowd blocks my view, and before I realize it, he's gone backstage again.

At the finale, all the acts come together to sing "We Are Family." Chantal sings directly to me before bowing and leaving the stage.

DeShawn and I stand there clapping long after all the acts leave the stage until finally, he leads me back to the dressing rooms to wait for Chantal. I'm a bundle of nervous energy, biding my time. When he emerges, looking as he did at dinner, I run at him, enfolding him in my embrace.

"You are breathtaking. I'm so happy you invited me."

"You think so?"

He lets go and steps back with a squeeze of my hand.

"You make a handsome man, but an even more breathtaking woman."

"Quit giving him a swole head and let's get outta here before someone tries to take me home," DeShawn interjects.

On the drive home, the boys and I rap along to various songs. This night is what I needed to clear my head and my heart feels full as we all get out of Chantal's car in front of the apartment complex.

DeShawn gives me a hug, before fist bumping Chantal. "I'm out."

Climbing the stairs, I try to stifle a yawn, but Chantal sees me even though I try to smother it behind my hand.

"Night, Ray," he says, kissing my cheek before walking to his apartment.

With a wave, I let myself into my apartment, locking the door behind me. Phone in hand, I throw down my purse and walk straight back to my room. Kicking off my shoes, I plug in my phone and fall into bed. There's a distinctive lump under the covers next to me, eliciting a scream. I'm about to wail on the lump when I hear Vonni's groggy voice.

"Jesus Christ, cara, it's me."

"Vonni, you scared the shit out of me. How did you get into my apartment?"

He yawns. "Aunt Carol's husband, Ray, taught me how to pick locks when I was ten."

"Ok." I'm not sure how to process this information. "Why are you in my bed?"

"I get my best sleep next to you." He grabs me, tucking me along his side and laying half on top of me. "Before you, I slept little."

With his head on my chest, he lets out a sigh. His breathing deepens as I play in his hair. It's true that it alarmed me to find Vonni in my bed, asleep, when I came home, but I must admit, now that he's here and my arms are around him, I don't mind so much. I suppose breaking and entering isn't that big of a deal to him, since he's fallen right back to sleep. Chantal's advice is in my head. Maybe I'll sleep on it and see if I still want Vonni in the morning. The answer is already in my heart as I drift off to sleep.

SIXTEEN

RACHAEL

My head pounds in time with my heartbeat as Vonni leans back for me to shut off my alarm. He makes himself comfortable on top of me as I shut my eyes, wishing I didn't have to go to work. Placing a hand on one of my breasts, he squeezes it through the corset I still have on. It's not the most comfortable garment, and right now I'm regretting being too tired and tipsy to take it off.

"I have to get up."

It's going to be a long day.

"Did you wear this out?" Vonni moves the covers back, looking down at my clothing. "I must have been pretty fucking tired not to notice."

"Chantal dressed me. Believe me, nobody batted an eyelash at what I was wearing at his club."

"I don't like you wearing lingerie, unless it's for me."

"Yeah, well, I don't like a man telling me what I can and can't wear."

I get out of bed, surprised when the pounding in my head

lessens when I stand. It's normally the opposite.

Pinching the bridge of his nose, he looks like he's praying for patience. "I didn't say you can't to wear it. I told you I don't like it. No guy wants other men fantasizing about their girl."

He sits on the edge of the bed, pulling me to him until I stand between his legs. He runs his hands up my legs, grabbing my butt under my skirt.

"In this outfit, you look good enough to eat."

I lean over, placing a light kiss on his forehead. "I have to get ready for work."

"Of course you do," he says, holding me for a minute more before he releases me.

Vonni's no longer in the bedroom when I get dressed, making me wonder if he left. The scent of coffee wafts down the hall as I make my way into the kitchen. He's sitting on a stool at the breakfast bar, looking quite at home. A cup of coffee sits in front of him as he eats a bowl of cereal while reading a text. Making myself a cup of coffee, I grab a yogurt from the fridge and stand across from him. A scowl disturbs his handsome features as he looks down at his phone.

"What's the matter?"

"It's nothing you need to worry about, cara." He puts his phone away and places his elbows on the counter, clasping his hands together. "Family business that will hopefully get resolved today."

Pulling out the drawer in front of me, I fish around inside of it until I find what I'm looking for, and then slide a key across the counter.

"So you don't get arrested for breaking into my apartment."

"We both know that's not something I'm likely to get arrested for." He crosses his arms over his chest, leaning back. "Are we going to talk about it?"

"What do you want from me?" I ask him, half dreading what his answer will be.

"What do you mean?"

"Am I the girl you call on a Saturday night because you're bored, or are you looking for something more serious?"

"I thought I made myself crystal clear." He meets my eyes across the counter. "You are mine. I don't share, and I don't play well with others."

"If we're going to be together, I have two conditions. First, there will be no mistresses on the side. Second, we never talk about the family business. You tell me on a need-to-know basis only. I'm a horrible liar. If I'm ever questioned, I want to have nothing to tell."

"Done." He nods, relaxing. "Tonight we're going to Nonno's place, so be ready at six." He gives me a lopsided smile. "Do you have any more outfits like the one you had on this morning?"

"I doubt I can wear anything like that to Nonno's." The thought of Nonno seeing me in the outfit I wore last night makes me cringe. "Are you trying to give the poor man a heart attack?"

"Nonno's place is a family hang out of sorts, not where he lives. I told everyone not to go by there. It will be just us, and George."

"I may regret asking this, but who is George?" I ask as I rinse out my dishes and put them in the dishwasher.

"George is a fixture around Nonno's. He's been with him since Pop was a kid."

Reaching over him for my purse, I brush my chest against him. "In that case, I'll wear something just for you."

His hand shoots out, grabbing me. Hungrily, he kisses me before letting go. On my way down the steps of my apartment, I decide Chantal's right; I think I can deal with things as they come.

SEVENTEEN

VONNI

Tapping my hand against my leg, I wait for Johnny and DJ to get into position. Sebastian reaches into the back seat of my SUV, pulling out his bat and laying it across his lap. The brick building across the street has a tattoo parlor on the lower floor, with apartments above. Judging by the run-down exterior, it's a shit hole inside. No place for a thirteen-year-old girl. If she's even here. Doesn't matter though, the man in apartment 2C will die today for his involvement.

Frankie Russo's grandson was kidnapped a month ago. He complied with all demands, paying the ransom to get the kid back. He was found a week later in a dumpster at the ripe old age of nineteen. Frankie's biggest mistake was failing to find the assholes responsible and killing them. They got away with a hefty sum of money. Why wouldn't they think they could hit one of the families again? The kidnapper's mistake was picking mine.

Seething, I think about my Aunt Jan's husband, Carlo. He's been a loyal soldier of my father's for years. His poor niece,

Kayla, has nothing to do with us. If I had my way, we'd get her back before our world taints her. That's the thing about innocence. Once it's gone, it's gone.

My phone beeps, and I look down with a smile. "They have the exits secured, let's go."

Sebastian nods, getting out of the car.

With my hands in my pockets, I casually cross the street. When I open the front door, I see another door on my left. The stencil lettering on the glass tells me it's the entrance to the tattoo parlor. A set of brown stairs is straight ahead and, taking them two at a time, I try to remain as quiet as possible. We have the element of surprise, but I'm not sure for how long. Sebastian and I move as a silent team down the dimly lit hallway, in front of apartment 2C, I pick both locks as quickly as I can. Drawing and cocking my gun, I slide the door open.

The sound of a TV from farther down the hallway is punctuated by a male cough. Not daring to open either door I pass in the hallway to look for Kayla, I continue. Sebastian taps me on the shoulder to let me know he's ready when we reach the end of the hallway. Stepping out of the shadows, I aim my gun at the shoulder of the man watching TV. Wouldn't do us any good to kill him right away in case our intel is wrong, and Kayla isn't being housed here.

Sebastian steps out from behind me, hitting his bat against the wall. The man jumps, his beady eyes on Sebastian. His hand goes for the gun on the couch next to him.

"Not so fast."

His eyes shift, noticing me for the first time. He raises his hands, knowing we got the drop on him. Sebastian swings the bat in his hands as he moves closer, drawing the guy's attention away from me. Still keeping my gun trained on him, I move toward the gun sitting on the couch. Sebastian hits him square in the stomach as I grab it. Sebastian takes zip ties out of his pocket and makes quick work of tying the guy's hands and ankles in front of him. Holstering my gun, I empty the other gun, putting it in my pocket.

An old plaid recliner sits next to the couch, with a rickety wooden end table between them. Sitting down in the recliner, I grab his hands, setting them down on the end table. From my pocket, I pull out a switchblade. Flicking it open, I stare at him.

"Do you know why we're here?" I ask, meeting his flat brown eyes head on.

"Why don't you enlighten me."

His faint Irish accent lets me know who I'm dealing with.

"Wrong answer." I slice the end of his pinkie off. He flinches but doesn't move. "Shall I take the next digit, or do you think you might need it?"

He spits at my shoes. "I'm not telling ye shit."

"I think he needs more motivation."

Sebastian looks around the room like he heard something. "I'm going to check the other rooms."

I slit into his pants with my knife, just to the left of his balls. "Maybe you care more about your dick than you do your fingers?"

"Fuck." A bead of sweat slips from his brow. "I didn't take her. I'm just supposed to keep her until I hear otherwise."

"Now we're getting somewhere. Give me names, and maybe you'll come out of this breathing."

"O-ok, I'll give you names, but we both know you ain't letting me walk out of here alive. I'll be damned if these arseholes get to go on living when I'm dead. Marcus and Keenan O'Bannon."

Pulling my gun from its holster, I put a bullet between his eyes. He's right, I would never let him live because that's not how shit is done in our world. Neither will the O'Bannon brothers. The kidnappings now make sense. The Irish Mafia is well known for having beef with the Italian Mafia. A feminine gasp from behind me has me hanging my head. Shit.

"Is he dead?" Kayla asks.

"Yes."

When I turn to meet her chocolate brown eyes, I don't

expect to see the hard glint in them. She moves closer, kicking the dead man's leg. She shocks me even further by throwing her long, dark hair over one shoulder to spit on him.

"A bullet is too good for him." She throws her arms around me, hugging me close. Her usual scent of oranges is replaced by cigarette smoke and sweat. "I knew the Morans would come for me."

I crush her slight frame against me as I tell her, "We protect our own."

"We got her," I hear Sebastian say from behind us. There's a brief silence before Sebastian appears on Kayla's other side. He nods at the dead man. "Did he give up who's involved?"

"Yeah. The O'Bannon brothers." I stand up, tucking Kayla against my side. "Tell Johnny and DJ to go hunting. Take out the O'Bannons only. I'd rather not start an all-out war if we can help it." With a sigh, I look at the man I just shot, then back at Sebastian. "Can you get the usual crew in here to clean up the mess?"

"Will do." Sebastian inclines his head toward Kayla. "Get her home. I'll catch a ride with Johnny."

Out of the corner of my eye, I watch Kayla on the way down the steps, expecting her to break down at any moment. Instead, she's stoic.

"Are you ok?"

It's a dumb question to ask and I regret it as soon as it leaves my lips. I just don't know what else to say to her.

"I will be." As I open her car door, she stands there looking at me. "Make sure you kill them all for me."

Shutting her car door behind her, I try not to let the shock I'm feeling register on my face. On the way to Carlo's house, what she said goes round and round in my mind. Our world has tainted her in a way that can't be undone, and I hate it. Even Mandy has a certain amount of innocence, and she was born into the same world I was.

Kayla runs toward Carlo without a backward glance as soon as I pull the SUV to a stop. He stands just inside the doorway, gripping her tightly. He looks at me over the top of her head with tears glistening in his eyes. In his heart, I know he never thought that Rafe's intel, Johnny's tracking skills, and DJ's stealth would be enough to bring her home alive. With a two-finger salute to Carlo, I pull away.

On the drive over to Rachael's, I think about her innocence and how much I crave it. She doesn't have any sinister plans or grand agendas when she looks at me. To her, I'm a man, just like any other. She's the light to my darkness.

My desire to lose myself in her overrides all else as I jog up the three flights to her apartment. When I open her door, I'm dumbstruck. Dumbstruck, then pissed.

EIGHTEEN

RACHAEL

Hurrying home after work, I text Chantal as soon as I get into my apartment. Hopefully, he's home, because I need help with my outfit and makeup. When he doesn't text me back after ten minutes, I decide to pour myself a glass of wine for courage and head into my closet.

My apartment door opens, and I hear what sounds like a troop of men coming in, then the door closing. I poke my head into the living room to find Chantal, DeShawn, and a group of strangers. DeShawn nudges Chantal after he notices me standing there.

"We were getting ready to go to my mom's for dinner when I got your text. I figured we'd come here on the way out."

"Who do you have with you?"

"The two on the end are my brothers, Dwayne and Kade." I step forward and shake hands with both. "The other three by DeShawn are my cousins Joe, Andre, and Terrell."

"Pleased to meet you, fellas." When I get to Terrell, instead of shaking my hand, he gives me a bear hug. "I appreciate you making a pit stop on the way out for me."

"Make yourselves comfortable. I'll be right back," Chantal says, with a general wave toward the group.

"See, I told you, cute little dark-haired girl," I hear DeShawn saying as we head back to my bedroom.

There's a collective mumble of agreement, which makes me chuckle.

Chantal closes the door before sitting on my bed and patting the spot next to him. "Dish while I do your makeup."

"When I came home last night, I found Vonni in my bed."

I smile, trying not to scrunch my eyes so he can work.

Chantal chuckles. "Oh damn, I like that kind of surprise."

"He fell back asleep, so the only thing I got was that he can pick locks. On the bright side, I knew I was right where I wanted to be as I fell asleep. This morning we had a talk, and I gave him two conditions. Monogamy, and I'm not involved in any part of the family business."

"Smart. I'm happy for you because I know he makes you happy." He gives me a sly look. "Now you mentioned slutty."

"He asked if I had any more clothes like I wore last night."

Chantal rifles through my drawers before pulling out a black silk spaghetti strap tank top. "What do you think of this green skirt with it?"

I stand next to him as he rifles through clothes. "It's his favorite color."

The skirt in question is a lighter emerald green color with a floral swirling pattern in a darker emerald green. I don't wear it often because it's shorter, and more fitted than I feel comfortable in at work.

"Put both on and let me see."

When I come out of the bathroom, Chantal looks me up and down. "Fierce. Put on the black cigar pumps with it."

I slide into them as he fastens a long, thin gold necklace that falls between my breasts. From the hallway, I hear the front door open and close.

Vonni's voice thunders from the front door. "What the

fuck is going on here?"

"Guys." DeShawn gives an uncomfortable cough. "This is Ray's man, Giovanni Moran."

When I walk into the living room, everyone turns toward me, staring.

"Shit, I'll wait for you guys outside," Andre says as he stands.

The room clears of all Chantal's family until the three of us are standing in the living room. Chantal's unfazed by the scowl on Vonni's face.

"Ray looks hot, doesn't she?" Chantal jabs Vonni in the ribs. "I'll just leave you two alone now."

He slides out the door, shutting it behind him.

Vonni's scowl transforms into a snarl. Crossing his arms, he glares at me.

"When I came to pick you up, I didn't expect to find a group of strange dudes hanging out in your living room." He gives my appearance a general wave with his hand. "And you come out of your bedroom looking like that!"

I mimic his earlier stance, crossing my arms over my chest and glaring right back at him. "Did you not ask me to wear an outfit like this for you?"

"For me, not half the apartment complex!"

Vonni closes his eyes, pinching the bridge of his nose.

"I asked Chantal if he had time to help me with an outfit and makeup. I didn't know until they came in that he had his brothers and cousins with him. They stopped on the way to Chantal's mom's house. You'll notice the only one in the bedroom with me would rather sleep with you than me."

"Great."

"I refrained from mentioning that you have a large, beautiful penis." I let my eyes wander from his face to his crotch and back up. "If you need me to, I can put in a kind word for you, though."

He stalks closer, his eyes straying to the tops of my breasts poking up from the corset. "You think my cock is beautiful?"

"I think it tastes even better than it looks."

I lick my lips, brushing my body along his. He goes to grab me, but I'm expecting his speed and sidestep him.

"After you feed me, of course." I head toward the door, turning to look over my shoulder. "I'm starving."

Vonni's silent, and a little surly on the ride over to Nonno's. Considering I probably left the guy with a giant hard-on, I don't take offense. He still runs his fingers along the length of my hand in the car, just like normal. Hopefully, this means he's not planning on holding a grudge.

The driveway at Nonno's place is gravel and walking on that with heels is going to be a nightmare. Vonni realizes my predicament and comes around to my side of the car to help support me until we reach the sidewalk. On the walk to the front door, I make him stop at the tree beside the house. I run my hands over a carving of a heart with the initials GM and RM inside.

"Those are my grandparents' initials. I'm named after Nonno, and my Nonna's name was Raine." He gives me a half smile. "When Chantal calls you Ray, it trips me up a bit."

The white paint on the clapboard exterior is chipping, giving the place an overall appearance of being old and worn. One black shutter seems to hang on by a thread. It's not at all what I was expecting.

"Wait until you see the inside." Vonni clears his throat. "Nonno keeps the outside looking a little rough to keep people away."

While the outside appears to be unloved, the inside is rich and masculine. All exposed brick, light colored wood, and black accents that blend expertly into the decor. Vonni steers me from the small entryway into a long room that has a bar on one end and a fireplace on the other. An older man with thick white hair stands behind the bar, nodding to us as we approach.

"George, this is Rachael," Vonni says, as we sidle up to the bar.

George's hands are warm and weathered as they envelop mine and his kind brown eyes twinkle under his bushy white eyebrows.

"What can I get you guys to drink?"

"If you can bring a bottle of wine to the table with dinner, that would be much appreciated."

Vonni steers me toward the fireplace where a small round table with a white tablecloth sits. Brushing his hand along my back, he pulls out my chair. He takes his seat across from me as George comes around with a pushcart. He pours two glasses of wine before setting the bottle on the table. With a flourish, he places two covered trays in front of us, removing both covers. The smell I love so much hits me.

"Vietnamese soup."

"I thought you might like it," Vonni says, with a small smile. "George picked it up instead of making us something."

"Thank you so much, George."

With a slight tilt of his head, he goes back to the bar.

"It's delicious, and I haven't had it in so long." Vonni raises an eyebrow at the low moan that escapes my lips. "Thanks for the surprise."

"My pleasure."

He sits there watching me eat for a minute before taking a spoonful himself. We eat in silence as I mull over what I want to say as Mandy's words come back to me. I'm pretty sure he will not take it well.

"Do you remember when you told me girls were attracted to you because of who your family is?"

"Yeah," he says, putting his spoon down.

"Let's say for argument's sake you had been born a girl. The reverse might be true. No guys would want to come within ten feet of you. It might be lonelier to have nobody want you at all, than to have someone sleep with you for the wrong reason."

He puts his hands flat against the table as his back goes rigid. "Where are you going with this?"

"I want to ask you for Sebastian's number so I can set him up with Mandy."

I eye him, waiting for an explosive reaction.

"Have you lost your mind?" His voice is controlled, making it even more menacing. "I'd kill him first."

"It's going to get pretty inconvenient to hide all the bodies of men who may or may not sleep with your sister. She deserves to be happy. Having seen what's out there, I'd say she could do a sight worse than Sebastian. At least he'll protect her and treat her like she deserves to be treated."

He narrows his eyes. "What makes you think he'll treat her well?"

With a deep breath, I get ready to drop a bomb on my poor, oblivious Vonni.

"Because he's in love with her."

"Did he tell you that?"

"He didn't have to. All you have to do is watch how he looks at her. How protective he is of her. All I'm asking is for you to consider that you might make two lonely people that you care about happy."

"Now I understand why Seb said you were going to be a handful." He leans back in his chair and steeples his fingers. "You don't even flinch when I'm pissed off."

"Mandy and I are a handful, are we? I suppose worse could be said about me." One of my eyebrows shoots up. "Should I be flinching?"

One corner of his lip twitches. "Most people do."

"I've had lots of male friends, and even more male coworkers over the years. All men are capable of violence, but some enjoy it. Even get off on hurting others. You're not one of those men that enjoys violence, even though it's part of your everyday life. This won't be the last time I piss you off, and no, I'm not worried about it."

"Speaking of Mandy, she asked me to give you this."

He reaches into his pants pocket, pulling out a padded envelope. When I open it, a stunning bracelet slides out. Two silver hearts sit at the center, with crystals surrounding them.

"It's beautiful."

"Jewelry making is her hobby. It's a friendship bracelet. I think the heart represents your budding friendship or something. I stopped listening to her explain the details after a while," he says with a devilish smirk.

It's the most heartfelt present I have ever received. Moisture appears at the corner of my eye that I try to wipe away before Vonni sees it. He leans forward, taking the bracelet out of my hand to put it on.

"Why are you crying, cara?"

Damn, I wasn't fast enough.

"I'm ruining Chantal's makeup."

I take my napkin, blotting underneath my eyes.

"Fuck the makeup, why are you crying?"

"These are happy tears, Vonni, calm down. It's such a thoughtful gift. She gave me her number before I left Sunday. I'll call her later and thank her."

He leans back in his chair, satisfied that all is well, and I change the subject before I cry in my soup.

"You remember the day we met?"

"Of course." He takes a bite of his soup. "I remember everything about you."

"Hmm, I'll come back to that in a minute. I think the girl that was sitting at the counter in the diner is a cop."

"FBI, actually. She's new, but the guy dressed like a biker is a veteran. What made you think she's a cop?"

"She paid special attention to you and Christian. It was what made me notice you to begin with. I was trying to put together what she found so interesting." I shake my head. "Wait, you knew who they were all long?"

"Being under constant surveillance is nothing new to us." One corner of his lip turns up. "I'm third generation, we know how to be seen and when to be seen. I will, however, have to go back and thank her for getting me the right attention for once."

"What do you remember about me from that night?"

I lean forward, curious about what he will say.

"You stared at my lips and hands with your beautiful brown eyes. I grew hard just from the way you watched me. You had on a blue T-shirt that stretched across your chest, making me think about how I'd like to bury my head there. In the light above your booth, your hair shone dark as midnight and looked so damn soft. I thought about how it would feel in my hands as I held your head against my aching cock."

He stands, adjusting himself before coming toward me. His hands have always held a certain fascination. The sight of him adjusting himself is such an enormous turn on that my eyes never leave his pants.

"I have something I want to show you."

He holds out his hand.

"I'll just bet you do."

He tugs me into the hall, turning away from the stairs as he leads me toward the back of the house. He opens a door, pulling me through it. Before I can even look around, he pushes me against the wall, shutting the door.

His lips are demanding and rough against mine. One of his hands slides up my leg, lifting both it and my skirt. My leg comes to rest against his hip. He moves his hand around to my butt, palming my cheek roughly. He rubs a finger between my thong and my butt before moving downward. Pushing the lace to one side, he torments my heated flesh with his finger before inserting it in me. The cool air against my most sensitive area causes me to shiver, and I ride his hand, trying to relieve the ache deep inside of me. His hand leaves me, making me whimper against his lips. Feeling him tug on my thong, I hear a ripping sound.

"Did you just rip my underwear?"

"They were in my fucking way." He pants. "I'll buy you more."

He moves back just enough to undo the button and zipper on his pants, pushing them down to just above his knees.

Never releasing the leg that rests on his hip, he murmurs against my ear.

"I'm so hard it hurts cara, tell me you ache for my cock."

"Fuck me hard, Von."

With a groan, he positions himself at my entrance, thrusting deep inside. He pumps in and out of me hard and fast. Placing his lips at the spot where my neck and shoulder meet, he sucks hard. On a long moan, I shatter, shivering around his cock. He thrusts deeply one last time before I feel his whole body shake with the force of his release.

Running his hand down my leg, I shiver as he pulls it from around him. He bends down to pick up the scrap of my thong that's left, putting it in his pocket. His cocky grin of satisfaction at seeing my clothes rumpled makes my heart flutter.

As I right my clothes, I look around the room. Brown leather loveseats are positioned across from each other in front of a large oak desk.

"Whose study is this?"

"It was Nonno's back when he bought this place. My father spent his early years here. When Nonno bought a bigger place, he turned this one into a family hang out. There are multiple bedrooms upstairs that any Moran can stay in when they need it."

I run my hand down a row of books on one bookshelf, perusing the titles. Nonno must be an avid reader to have accumulated this many books. There are classics like The Great Gatsby, mixed in with mysteries and crime thrillers. Vonni must have sensed I'd be lost in here for days because he came up behind me, putting his arms around me.

"Let's go home, cara," he says, grabbing my hand and leading me back out.

Vonni waves as he passes the bar on the way out. "See you later, George."

"It was nice to meet you, George." Vonni tugs on my hand as I call out, "Thanks for everything!"

Steadying me as we make our way back to the car, he lifts me in, palming my bare ass. He climbs in, playing with his phone until music fills the car. He rubs along each individual finger of my hand as he drives. With my head leaning against the leather seat, I relax on the way back to my apartment.

My phone rings as we're getting out of the car, and I look down at the display. Damn if I don't miss the sound of my cousin Kevin's voice. Eagerly, I push the button to answer it.

"Hey, what's up?"

"I was wondering how things are going with Kendra?"

"You failed to mention dating her for an entire year," I say as Vonni and I climb the stairs side by side. "You don't date anyone that long."

He chuckles. "Every hound dog occasionally lingers."

Vonni steps around me, using his key to let us in.

"She's hot. I didn't know you could get high-quality tail like that. I thought it was just skanks and weirdos."

"Hilarious, asshole. She's hot, but she was also a high maintenance pain in the ass. Not that she didn't have her good points. She was adventurous in bed, and she never tried to change me."

"What happened then?"

I sit on the sofa and take off my pumps.

"Many containers come and go all the time from the docks. One day I was checking a row of containers before they were due to be loaded on the ship. One container had a broken seal. Upon further inspection, I saw someone had tampered with the latch. I opened it to make sure nothing was damaged. There were a couple of high-end cars in it, still in mint condition. I closed the container and reported it to Kendra's father. He said he was going to take care of it."

He pauses. "That seemed weird. Why didn't he just say it was fine, seal it back up? I had a feeling something was up, but I couldn't put my finger on it. It bugged me so much I went back and questioned him further about it. He told me to forget what I saw. I got this uneasy sense that I stumbled upon something I shouldn't have. Like Kendra's dad was mixed up in something. It made me uncomfortable, so I left the city and came home."

"And knowing all that, you got me a job there?"

"You're in the office, not on the docks." He huffs out a breath. "Who knows, it could have been just one container of stolen cars. Someone may have been fired, which is why he told me he'd take care of it. I know nothing for certain. Maybe I was making it into a bigger deal than what it was because a part of me was looking for an excuse to bail on her. Things were getting too serious."

That is more of a believable reason than what he was saying before.

"Well, she doesn't seem to have held a grudge. Dragon Lady has been cool."

"Have you met a guy named Christian at the docks?" he asks, a note of suspicion coloring his voice.

"Yeah, he seems cool."

Damn Kevin for picking up on Christian's name for Kendra.

"I want you to listen to me. Stay away from any guys with the last name Moran. Hell, stay away from any guys who are affiliated with them."

"Noted." I don't have the heart to tell him his warning is a little too late. "Listen, I'm going to settle in for the night. I'll talk to you later."

"Ok, but make sure you stay away from Christian."

"I can take care of myself."

Christian isn't the Moran he needs to worry about.

"Your cousin is worried about you at the docks?"

"Not exactly. He wants me to stay away from the Morans, Christian specifically."

"That's excellent advice." He laughs. "I'm not sure which one is worse, Christian or Rafe. I field calls daily from girls they are avoiding."

"They don't field calls for you?"

"No, cara, they don't. I have more responsibilities than they do. They can enjoy certain benefits that come with the name, that are unwise in my position. I won't paint myself as a monk, but women always knew what they were getting. Besides, everyone knows I'm not the most handsome of the Morans. There's a reason women flock to Christian and Rafe."

I let my eyes wander over his body. "You're the sexiest of the Morans."

"I better be the only man you're looking at." He leans forward, his breath fanning my neck. "Come on, let's go watch a movie in bed."

"Oh, is that what they're calling it these days?"

NINETEEN

VONNI

Sebastian groans. "Why are you calling me so early?"

"Get your ass up, sunshine." Sebastian has never been a morning person, and I enjoy fucking with him a little. "You'll be taking over for me on the docks, as of this morning."

"You really must hate me to call me at the crack of dawn, just to tell me I have to deal with Dragon Lady."

"I need someone I can trust with the family's business on the docks, that can also handle Kendra. Fuck if I know why, but Rachael enjoys working for her. My presence down there will only cause her problems."

"Who are you going to get to run the protection rackets?"

He moves around like he's getting ready while we're talking.

"I think Luke can handle it, don't you?"

"Yeah, he'll be fine." I hear water running in the background. "He's got a good handle on when to help, and when to get rough and tumble."

"Good. After you check in with Kendra, go see Rachael. She

has something she wants to talk to you about."

"We won't be braiding each other's hair or some shit by the end of this talk, will we?"

"Maybe, if you had any hair." I run down the front steps of my brownstone. "One last thing Seb."

"What?"

I smile at the dread in his tone.

"I spoke with Pop and Nonno earlier this morning. They are making an exception to Nonno's family rule. You've more than proven yourself over the years. Congratulations, you're being promoted to capo."

The whoop he lets out is so loud I have to hold the phone away from my ear. Getting into Luke's Mustang, I hang up, a smile still on my face.

Luke's never been a chatty kid, but today he's downright stoic as he drives toward the garment district. I watch his profile, considering whether I want to know what's wrong with him. A muscle ticks in his jaw, a worse sign than his ears being red in frustration. Fuck me, my day started off so well.

"Why are you so pissed?" His jaw clenches, but he doesn't say a word. "Girl trouble?"

"You got that fucking right, girls are trouble."

"I threw my phone into the floorboard so hard it put a crack in the screen when Rachael wasn't talking to me."

"That's not like you at all."

He pulls up to the curb, sitting there instead of getting out.

"No, it's not." I look out the window, watching the throng of people moving along the sidewalk. Racks of clothes are being pushed back and forth across the street. "Caring about a woman is frustrating as hell."

"Tell me about it. She's not talking to me. I went to that party, threw her over my shoulder, and left. Guys take advantage of drunk girls at those parties. I'll be damned if I have to kill a fucker, because they laid a hand on her."

"Why didn't you just go to the party with her?"

I'm curious why this solution didn't seem to occur to

Luke.

"Because I'm twenty-one." He's looking at me like I have three heads. "I don't want to go to a party thrown by high schoolers."

"Yes, you are past that part of your life, but she isn't." I let that statement sit there for a second. "If you want to keep her, once in a while you are going to have to do things you don't want to do."

I could tell by his blank stare he doesn't quite understand what I'm trying to say.

"For example, I had George pick up Vietnamese soup for Rachael. She loves the stuff. Frankly, I was prepared to eat something I hated. Thankfully, it tasted good even though it smelled god-awful."

"That worked for you, huh?"

"I fucked her up against the wall in Nonno's old office." I meet his gaze and open my door. "Whereas your ass is still in the doghouse. You tell me."

Making my way through the throng of people on the sidewalk, I enter my Aunt Ashley's shop. There are bolts of fabric everywhere you turn, intersected with mannequins displaying different outfits. The fabric displays end at a row of dressing rooms. Ashley's assistant, May, stands in front of a mannequin playing with a piece of fabric that looks like it will one day become a shirt.

"That color is all wrong for the skirt."

I smirk, watching her take a pin out of her mouth and insert it.

"If Christian had told me that, I'd switch out the fabric." Her almond-shaped brown eyes narrow to slits. "For you, maybe I stick you with a pin." The corner of her eyes crinkles as a smile breaks out across her face. "Why haven't you come to see me in so long?"

I move closer to kiss the top of her head. Her once jet-black hair is now sprinkled with gray. She still wears her hair in the same bob she's had since I was a teenager. Despite her small stature, she's a force to be reckoned with. She doesn't take crap from anyone, least of all our family. Her respect in the garment district, and more important in our family, is widely known. She keeps a keen eye out for my aunt, who remains oblivious to our family's activities.

"Pop's been keeping me busier than usual."

"Pop or your girlfriend?" She pats me on the cheek. "Ashley couldn't wait to tell me Monday morning."

"Both. How's business?"

"We're right on track. The truck will be here shortly to load everything. Come, tell me what you think of something I've been working on."

Following her into the back, I wonder what's keeping Luke. Normally, Christian comes with me. He enjoys coming down to the garment district, which feeds into his love of both fashion and women. Today, however, I need Christian to help DJ and Johnny with their pursuit of the O'Bannon brothers. Violence is a part of our world, but we avoid it at all costs with women. That's where Christian shines. Between his good looks and charm, there aren't too many women who can resist him.

My aunt is bent over a sewing machine, cursing at a dress. May continues past her to a row of metal racking. Purses of every size and assortment are shoved in the cubbies. She pulls out a bag, handing it to me.

"Is it real or fake?"

I inspect the bag, looking for all the telltale signs of a fake. Christian might have a better fashion sense than me, but nobody is better at spotting a fake than me. Especially not a Louis Vuitton. It's my only claim to luxury. If they make it for men, I have it.

"You almost had me with this one, May. All you're missing is a date code on the inside of the bag. Are these going uptown with the street vendors?"

The city is known for selling knockoff bags. May has quite the side hustle going on, which, of course, we get a piece of.

There's not too much that goes on in this city that we don't get a piece of.

"Drat." She shakes her head, her shoulders slumping. "I knew if anyone could tell me where I went wrong, it would be you."

"I told you he would spot it," Ashley speaks up from behind us, her head still bent over the sewing machine.

Luke strides in, a big grin stretching across his face. He comes up to May, lifting her into the air and swinging her around.

"Boy, put me down."

She swats at him until he sets her back down.

Crossing my arms over my chest, I stare at him. "You're in a better mood."

"Got everything straightened out," he says, inclining his head toward Ashley.

Part of me considers messing with him, but then I'd only have to deal with his sour mood the rest of the day. It's just not worth it. Movement from the doorway catches my eye. A tall gaunt man wearing our trucking company's T-shirt stands there looking unsure whether he should interrupt.

"Let's help him load up," I say, hitting Luke in the chest on my way past him.

TWENTY

RACHAEL

Standing in line at Starbucks, I wait on my large coffee, Kendra's espresso, and Sam's mocha latte to be made. It's been my experience that it never hurts to get in good with either your boss or the security guard. However, patience has never been my strong suit. I'm tapping my nails on the counter when I feel someone come up behind me. Turning around, I see Sebastian smiling down at me.

"I thought that was you with the annoying tapping."

Today he's wearing a white T-shirt with his standard cross and jeans. It's interesting that he's the only one of John's guys that dresses casually.

"I know it's shocking that I lack patience. What are you doing here this morning?"

"I'm getting my fix before I head over to the docks," Sebastian says, holding up a large coffee cup.

"Me too. In this case, I'm also a supplier for Kendra and Sam." When the barista calls out my name, I grab my order from her. "I thought Vonni and Christian come to the docks?"

"Vonni thought it would be best if I take over from now on." Sebastian holds the door open for me. "Being that you're in a relationship, he didn't want that to interfere with your job. I hear through the grapevine that Kevin wants you to stay away from Christian."

"Where are you parked?" I ask as we walk down the sidewalk.

He nods toward a sleek black Charger.

"My cousin wants me to stay away from all Morans, including anyone that's with a Moran. That ship has long since sailed."

"I'd say so." He laughs. "I think Vonni has ulterior motives for keeping Christian away from you."

"I don't doubt that." I set my order on top of the Jeep while I throw my purse in. "See you over there, ok?"

He walks over to his car with a wave of his hand. Before he gets in, he turns around.

"You should put that coffee in your car." He smirks. "Hate for you to get back with no coffee."

With a roll of my eyes, I flip him the bird.

Sebastian is already waiting on the sidewalk when I pull in. We walk in side by side, making a pit stop at the security desk to hand Sam his cup.

"Morning, Sam, special delivery."

"You're a doll." He's an imposing figure, even with a wide grin. "No one ever asks if I want coffee."

"Today's your lucky day then," I tell him, walking backward toward the elevators.

When we get off the elevator, I turn to Sebastian. "I'm guessing you're here for Kendra, if you'd do me a favor and bring her a coffee."

"Yeah, I'll meet with her, then come back and talk to you." He reaches out, taking the coffee from me. "Vonni says there's something you want to talk to me about."

As I watch him walk toward Kendra's office, I'm a little shocked. It must be about Mandy. I must have gotten through

117

to Vonni after all.

I'm staring at my computer screen when Sebastian raps his knuckles on my door before walking in. He shuts the door behind him, sitting down across from me. When I don't start talking, he picks at the fabric of his jeans.

"So, what did you want to talk to me about?"

"Don't look so worried. At dinner last night, I asked Vonni for your number to talk to you about Mandy."

He sits forward, resting his elbows on his knees. "What's wrong with Mandy?"

"Nothing is wrong with Mandy," I tell him, not wanting him to stroke out before I even get started. Letting him lean back and get comfortable in his chair, I continue, "Mandy is a pretty girl."

"She is, what's your point?"

"My point is, you should ask her out."

"On a date," he chokes out. "Vonni said it was ok for me to go on a date with his sister?"

"He blustered for a minute, but you're here talking to me, aren't you?"

He sits with his hand resting against his mouth, and his leg jiggling. "Let me get this straight. You asked Vonni if you could talk to me about dating Mandy."

"The men in the Moran family don't understand what it's like for Mandy. She has to deal with men being too scared to ask her out. That's even lonelier than having someone sleep with you for the wrong reasons. You're from her world, you can protect her. I also think you care for her, which means you'll treat her well. I care very much about Mandy's happiness. That being said, if you hurt her, I'll cut off your penis and throw it off the docks."

"Fair enough." He inclines his head at my wrist. "Did Mandy make you that bracelet?"

"Isn't it beautiful?" I smile down at my bracelet. "Vonni says it's a friendship bracelet."

"When she was eighteen, she bought me this cross to keep

me safe." He looks down at the heavy cross hanging from his neck. "I haven't taken it off since."

"Get out of my office and go ask Mandy out. I'm sure you know where she is right now."

He stands up, smirking down at me, before leaving without saying a word.

Grabbing my phone, I text Mandy.

ME: Lunch today?

MANDY: Sure. Somewhere close to the docks? Maybe seafood?

ME: I love seafood. Text me the name of the place. I'll meet you over there at one.

MANDY: I'm excited! I'll see you over at The Fish Shack.

Feeling very pleased with myself, I put my phone away and resume work. Before I know it, it's almost one and I'm rushing out the door of my office. I pause at the guard desk on my way out.

"Sam, how do I get to The Fish Shack?"

His surly demeanor vanishes as he smiles at me. "Sure thing. Hang a left out of the parking lot. Drive two blocks, and it's on the corner. Can't miss it."

The Fish Shack is, in fact, a wooden structure that faces the water. The white sign out front outlines an angler casting a line.

When I walk in, I see Mandy already sitting in a wooden booth facing the water. The tabletops are all steel, and the place has that look like you can throw peanut shells on the floor. Our server must have caught her waving because he arrives at the table at the same time I do. He barely looks old enough to work.

His chin length blond hair falls in his face, partially covering his green eyes. "What can I get you ladies to drink?"

"Water for me," Mandy says.

"I'll take a Coke, thanks."

Our server isn't even out of earshot when Mandy starts talking, "Sebastian came by the house this morning!" She bounces up and down in her seat. "He asked me to dinner tonight!"

"I may have spoken with him this morning," I tell her with a grin that would put the Grinch to shame.

She wags her finger in my direction. "I knew it!"

"What should I get?"

"I picked this place because it's all good." She sits with her head in her hands. "Now, give me all the details."

The server sets our drinks down in front of us. "Do you ladies know what you'd like to order?"

"I'll have the fried shrimp."

"Scallop risotto for me," I say, handing the server my menu.

Once he's out of earshot, I continue, "It all started at dinner last night. I pointed out to Vonni that it must be lonely not having anyone brave enough to ask you out because of who your family is. I mentioned you could do worse than Sebastian, and he could make two people he loves happy. After he thought it over, he must have decided I had a point because he sent Sebastian to see me this morning. I'm glad to see Sebastian took me literally when I told him to leave my office and ask you out. Of course, I may have threatened to cut off his penis and feed it to the sharks if he ever hurt you."

"I doubt Seb has ever had anyone threaten his penis before." She giggles. "I would have loved to have seen the look on his face."

"He's a good sport, but I didn't invite you to lunch to talk about Sebastian. Thank you for my bracelet. It's the sweetest gift I have ever received."

"Vonni mentioned freaking out when you started crying. I'm very flattered that you like it that much."

"It's beautiful, Mandy." I reach across the table, squeezing her hand. "My favorite part is the hearts that represent us."

The server returns, setting our plates in front of us.

"OMG, Mandy, this is so good."

"Told you. I hear your cousin doesn't want you around us,

especially Christian."

I grin. "If he only knew that Christian isn't the Moran he needs to keep me away from."

"Vonni will never give you up. He's in love with you."

She makes an *O* with her lips before covering her mouth with her hands.

"You're wrong! We haven't been together long enough."

"Since when does love make sense?" She shrugs her shoulders. "Nonno knew Nonna was the one for him on their first date. That's saying something, considering he was known for being a bit of a player. My parents were married after only six months, and they still gross me out."

"I-I have to get back to work, Mandy," I say, looking down at my phone and noticing how late it's getting to be. "Lots to get done today."

Signaling the server, I give him my credit card to speed things along. When he comes back with my card, we stand up, walking side by side out of the restaurant.

"I had fun." On the sidewalk, she embraces me. "Thanks for lunch."

"Call me and let me know how it goes with Sebastian."

She blushes, heading off in the opposite direction. I make a mad dash for the car, driving back as fast as I safely can. I'm in a rush, not paying attention to my surroundings. Not surprisingly, I run smack into something. Not something, someone. A thick chest, to be exact. I'm about to say sorry, but the words die in my throat. The man towering over me is none other than my ex-husband, looking like he hasn't aged a day.

"What are you doing here?"

I meet his sky blue eyes with an angry glare. How dare he randomly just show up at my job?

"You look good," he says, giving me a slow once over. "Nancy at the plant told me you were working here. Since I had a few days off, I thought I'd stop by."

I make a mental note to ask Kevin to have a talk with Nancy. The last thing in the world I want is my ex tracking me down. Looking down at my phone, I see I'm running late and thus don't have time for his nonsense. When I try to step around him, he moves to block me. He reaches out, grabbing my arm.

"Dan, it's not appropriate for you to show up at my job. Now drop my arm and let me by." I give him my best piercing stare. "I'm late coming back from lunch."

He smiles down at me, staying where he is. I bring my knee into his groin hard, moving around him while he's bent over in pain. Sam is already halfway to me and walking even faster. Several of the dock workers have stopped what they are doing to stare. A few of them head toward me.

"I saw him grab your arm, and I hurried out," Sam says, eyeing Dan, who is still bent over and groaning.

"Thanks for the backup, Sam. He'll leave as soon as his balls recover."

Sam whistles low and laughs. A small crowd of guys from the docks has come up to us, to which I mentally groan.

"Everything's fine, guys," Sam addresses the group. "She got the drop on her unwanted visitor."

All the men look behind us at my ex-husband, then back at me with wide eyes.

"Fellas if you'll excuse me, I'm late coming back."

Without a backward glance, I head inside, but no sooner have I sat down at my desk to clock back in, when my phone rings. When I look at the caller ID, I sigh.

"Hey."

"Are you ok?" Vonni asks.

"Boy, word travels fast around here." I drum my nails on the desk. "It's nothing, I took care of it."

"Cara, what happened?"

"My ex-husband appeared out of the blue. When he was trying to talk to me in the parking lot, he grabbed my arm. I didn't have time for his line of bullshit, so I kicked him in the nuts. Let me go, I have a lot to get done today."

"All right, bruiser, I'll let you get back to work," he says with a chuckle.

The rest of my workday flies by without incident. Before I know it, five o'clock has arrived. Shutting off my computer, I throw my phone in my purse. Kendra stands in my doorway, with her purse on her shoulder, smiling.

"I heard there was a scuffle in the parking lot. Word on the street is you dropped a big dude. It's giving you quite the reputation on the docks."

"I would rather nobody saw that."

I grab my purse and walk out with her.

"Ex-boyfriend?" she asks, as we ride the elevator down.

"Worse. Ex-husband. I don't know why he showed up after all this time. You have my word. He won't be a problem."

"Oh, I'm more worried about his safety than anything else." She waves over the top of her car in the parking lot. "Have a good night."

"See you in the morning."

On my ride home, I wonder why Dan appeared again after all this time. True, when we lived in the same small town, he would try to win me back with no success. Why try when I live six hours away? Still pondering things as I reach the top of my stairs, my phone rings.

"Cara, something's come up." Vonni's voice has an odd hitch to it. "I won't be home until late."

"Vonni."

I close the door to my apartment behind me.

"Yes, cara."

"You'll be careful, won't you," I choke out.

"I could get used to having you worry over me."

"Will it hurry you along if I say I'll be waiting for you naked in bed?"

"I will come back to you as quickly as I can," he growls. "I have to go now, cara, they are waiting for me."

After he hangs up, I stare at the phone, trying to hold myself together. Dread sits in the pit of my stomach. We agreed to keep family business on a need-to-know basis. I'm wondering if that was smart of me. I was only thinking of my inability to lie with a straight face. Now I'm wondering if I should reconsider. Is it better to know the danger ahead of time, or deal with the aftermath? No, I can't think that way. For my sanity, I will carry on as normally as possible.

The most normal thing I can do is order in Chinese and throw on my sweats. I pour a glass of wine and flip through the channels. Nothing holds my attention for long, and at ten I decide to go to bed. I toss and turn, falling into a fitful sleep.

That night, I dream about grotesque demons coming after Vonni. No matter how hard I try to save him, I'm too late to stop them from killing him. I lie in a crumpled heap, helplessly watching him die over and over. Screams of sorrow and terror fill me.

TWENTY-ONE

VONNI

Nonno and Lorenzo Bianchi have always shared similar views on how they run their respective families. When Pop took over for Nonno, he kept everything the same. There is a reason behind every rule Nonno had. The most important rule, only trust family. If you aren't related, you don't get close to the family or the business. The same can be said for Lorenzo Bianchi. Both families have no choice but to enlist lower-level soldiers, however, every segment of the total operation is overseen by a family member.

You can't ascend to the rank of capo or above without being related. The only exception in either family is Sebastian. My argument, in Sebastian's case, is very compelling. Sebastian's father had given up his life in the service of our family. Sebastian himself has taken a bullet. In my mind, there's no question that Sebastian's loyalty can never be bought. Even after all of that, to be honest, I never expected the answer to be yes.

Nonno's second most important rule, the sale of drugs,

is forbidden for everyone across the board. The penalty for being caught breaking this rule is death. He felt it attracted too much unwanted police attention. The Morans and the Bianchis are the only families that abstain from the very lucrative drug trade. I've seen the havoc drugs wreak in the other families, and I have to agree with Nonno.

Information is its own currency in our world, and my brother Rafe is the king. He can find out anything about anyone. He helped to pursue Kayla, having the apartment address within a day and a half of her being taken. This time, however, the information he has means death for one of our soldiers and one of the Bianchis.

Johnny tracked the two men to a warehouse in the Bronx. DJ already snuck in and confirmed the two men are inside, but they aren't alone. A heavily armed guard is standing watch at both points of entry and men patrol along the inside of the warehouse. The men we are after are standing in the main section of the warehouse, surrounded by armed guards. DJ estimates that there are twelve men in the warehouse.

Pop sits next to me in the front seat of my SUV, rubbing his jaw. Turning around, he looks at Lorenzo sitting in the back seat with his eyebrow raised. Lorenzo's eldest son, Marco, sighs from the seat next to him. None of us like what we're seeing. From the looks of things, they are expecting company, which can only mean that someone tipped them off. Even if we don't strike now, we'll never have the element of surprise.

"I don't like it, but what other choice do we have, John?" Lorenzo stares out the car window at the darkened husk of the warehouse. "I'm surprised an operation of this size hasn't already brought the cops down on us."

"I agree." Pop sighs, giving me a nod. "Set the plan in motion."

Taking my phone out of my breast pocket, I send a text letting everyone know we are a go. Two-man teams are already formed, with a member of the Bianchi family being paired with a member from our family. It's just a matter of everyone getting into position.

DJ, and Marco's younger brother Nico, are sent in ahead of time to get into position. Their job is to offer us cover in the main section of the warehouse where there is a higher concentration of men. Sebastian's team will take one exit, while Christian's takes the other. The rest of the teams will follow them in, eliminating men as they go. Lorenzo and Marco will be the last ones through the side door, with Pop and I being the last ones going in through the front door.

The sound of gunfire already echoes in the warehouse by the time Pop, and I are at the front door, ready to enter. I put my hand on Pop's arm, holding him back so I can go in ahead of him. The entry to the warehouse is small and dimly lit, with a hallway branching off either side of it. Figuring that the left side leads around to where Marco is coming in from, I go right. I can see a form lying on the cement floor up ahead. As I stoop next to the body, I see it's not one of our guys. By the time I make it around to the main section of the warehouse, I pass three bodies, thankfully none of them ours.

Long windows line the top of this section, almost at the roofline. In the hallway, there are only large hanging lamps every so often, and in this section, there is an abundance of fluorescent lights. Crouching down, I peek my head around the corner to assess the situation. What I see makes my heart stop.

Marco and Lorenzo are pinned down in a hail of gunfire across the warehouse, trying to take cover behind a steel pole. They alternate positions, one leaning out and shooting while the other stays behind the pole. It can't last, one or both will run out of bullets. Staying low, I skirt along the side wall so I can sneak up behind the shooters. When I hear gunfire from close behind me, I know Pop is covering my back. DJ and Nico take a few shots from above before having to seek cover themselves. They give me the distraction I need to make my move.

Two bullets find their mark simultaneously. The man I

had been aiming at falls, but not before he fires one last bullet. Marco's strangled cry brings my attention back to him. He's sitting on the ground, bullets whizzing past him, holding Lorenzo in his arms. Rage clouds my judgment, bringing me out from my position of cover behind a table where they are growing marijuana. My father shouts from behind me, but it's no use. Pulling my second gun from my shoulder holster, I fire. By the time the last man shooting at Marco hits the floor, I'm already dropping to my knees beside him.

"No!" The scream is torn from Marco's very soul. "He can't be dead, Vonni, he can't!"

Lorenzo's sightless eyes stare up at me. In the wave of such deafening gunfire, it's suddenly quiet. When I stare into Marco's eyes, there's nothing I can say. Marco doesn't want to believe his father is gone, but we both know he is. All I can do is embrace him.

Looking up, I see Pop standing over us. His grief is written all over his face. Footsteps pound before Nico comes skidding to a stop, falling to his knees beside us. Nico's tan skin turns ghastly white as he takes in the sight of his brother holding their father. I scoot back to give the brothers a minute of privacy.

I stand to survey the room, needing to account for my family. Losing even one more person today is more than I can stomach. Death is an accepted part of our lives, but it still wears on me every time.

"Luke has a flesh wound that will need stitches." Sebastian's deep voice comes from my right. "Rafe just left to take Tommy and Jeff to the hospital. Nothing life threatening, but both will need medical attention."

"How about the Bianchis?"

"We're all accounted for," a stocky guy with short cropped red hair speaks up. I recognize him as being one of the Bianchi's newer soldiers. "Your brother Luke left with one of our guys who is wounded, but not critical."

"Good."

With a nod, he heads off to talk to the other Bianchi men. I tap Sebastian on the shoulder, inclining my head. Sebastian follows me off to the side and out of Marco's hearing. To be on the safe side, I lower my voice.

"Can you get our usual cleanup crew over here as soon as possible? Coordinate with Luca Bianchi and see if they can lend a hand. It's going to take a while, and I want it done before daylight."

Sebastian takes out his phone, heading off in the other direction. My heart sinks as I watch Marco and Nico work together to lift their father gently. Pop leads the way, and I fall in behind the Bianchi brothers, as if it were a formal funeral procession. To watch the men lower their heads before falling in behind me shows the level of respect they have for Lorenzo.

Rachael's smiling face fills my mind. Odd to think of that, when I can feel the Bianchi brother's sorrow as we walk out of the warehouse. Maybe it's how I'm coping with the fact that it could just as easily have been me carrying my father's body out the door. It could have been any of us.

TWENTY-TWO

RACHAEL

The sound of my alarm is annoying, and I feel like I've been run over by a truck. I wipe at the sleepy seeds in the corner of my eye and lean over to turn it off. My gaze lands on the empty spot where Vonni should be, and I can't draw in enough breath to fill my lungs.

Shooting out of bed like there's a mattress spring under my body, I get up and look in the bathroom, but he isn't there either. I run out to the living room searching for him, but I come up empty. My heart thunders in my chest, and my palms are damp as I charge into the kitchen.

There he is, at the coffeepot, doing something normal and mundane. With an unsteady breath, I devour him with my gaze. It feels like there's nothing more precious in that moment than the sight of his back, his muscles bunching under the shirt he's still wearing from yesterday. He turns around, and I notice a tiny drop of blood on the sleeve of his shirt. I don't care; I fly into his arms, sobbing uncontrollably.

"Cara, what's wrong?" he murmurs, hugging me tightly

and stroking my hair.

My entire body shakes as I bring my hands up between us, shoving his chest so hard he falls back a step.

"Are you fucking shitting me? When I couldn't find you this morning, I thought you were dead. Do you have any idea how terrified I've been sitting at home, while you were out doing god knows what?"

He steps closer and puts his arms around my waist, leaning the upper half of his body far enough away to look into my eyes.

"I didn't get home until four in the morning." He wipes away my tears with his thumb. "I knew I wouldn't be able to sleep, so I sat in the chair watching you. You looked so damn beautiful that it made my chest ache. Before your alarm went off, I got up to make coffee for you. Nothing short of death will keep me from being right next to you when you wake up from now on."

He bends forward, taking my face in his hands, and brushing his lips against mine. Moaning, he runs his tongue along the seam of my mouth. His tongue meets mine, playing for a minute before he sucks it into his mouth.

When I push against his arms with the flats of my hand, he releases my lips, but not my face.

I reach up and brush his bangs back. "I have to get ready for work."

"Of course you do," he says, bending forward to kiss me one last time before he drops his hands.

Needing to be alone, I lock the door behind me in the bathroom. Under the spray of the shower, I have a good long cry. When I wipe the steam from the bathroom mirror, I see I look like hell. My eyes are puffy, with dark circles under them. With a sigh, I open the door and go to my closet, but by the time I leave my bedroom I'm firmly in control of my emotions.

Taking a deep breath in, I head into the kitchen to face Vonni. He pours a cup of coffee into my travel mug, handing it to me. The thought of breakfast after all the emotional turmoil of the last twelve odd hours makes my stomach turn.

I paste on a fake smile and try to sound chipper. "I'm off to work."

"I have to go to a club for a meeting tonight." He lightly grabs my arm as I turn to leave. "I'm going to take you with me. We'll go out to dinner before we go."

With a nod, I leave.

On the drive to work, I force myself to face some hard truths. This morning when I thought I had lost Vonni, everything changed. I can no longer hide or deny my feelings, even to myself. I'm in love with him.

Vonni can't change the family he was born into. He will never turn his back on his family. Loyalty and family obligation made him into the man he is today, the man I love. If I'm going to be with him, I must accept the harsh realities that come along with that decision. He could end up being injured, incarcerated, or killed. This will have consequences for not only myself, but any children we may have. The bigger question is, can I ever live without him after knowing what it's like to live with him?

TWENTY-THREE

VONNI

Leaning against Luke's red Mustang, I watch him talk to Mr. Yankovic through the window of the bakery. All the businesses on this block have a similar look, brick buildings with glass fronts. Mostly they are small family-owned businesses run by immigrants. The people here don't turn to the cops when they have a break in, they call us. Doesn't matter if they need a loan or a business license, we take care of those things too.

The block's old-world feel makes it my favorite part of the city, and I want to share it with Rachael. Thinking about tonight, I pull out my phone and dial Sebastian. For her safety, I don't dare leave her by herself inside the club, and I can't take her with me inside Paul's office.

"The last time you called me, I ended up in a shootout. The time before that I was assigned Dragon Lady." He snorts. "I'm almost afraid to ask what you need me to do today."

"Well, hello to you too, asshole." I watch a group of four teenage boys surrounding one smaller Asian boy, forcing him into the alley next to The Golden Dragon. "I'm taking Rachael with me to the club tonight for my meeting with Paul."

Pushing off the car, I cross the street, moving toward the mouth of the alley. "Bring Mandy and we'll go to dinner first. Keep the girls' company while I'm in with Paul."

The Asian boy hunches over, holding his waist as the older kids yell racist comments.

"I'll grab Mandy and meet you at your place. What time?"

"Five thirty." The tallest of the teenagers shoves the Asian boy against the wall. "Seb, what does Mr. Woo's son look like?"

"He looks like a mini version of Mr. Woo. Even though he's twelve, he looks much younger because he's on the scrawny side. Why?"

"I think I just got the protection racket for The Golden Dragon. See you tonight."

Hanging up, I silently move down the alley. The sound of my gun cocking makes all the boys turn. They shift uneasily, looking at each other. Everyone except the stocky kid still holding the Asian boy by his shirt collar. Wild guess says he's the ringleader of this shitshow.

"Everybody, except you." I point at the ringleader. "Beat it."

The rest of the boys take off at a dead run out of the mouth of the alley, disappearing without a backward glance. Recognition lights the Asian boy's face, and his eyes go wide.

"Are you Mr. Woo's son?"

"Y-ye-yes."

"What's your name?"

"W-Wi-William."

"Hello, William, I'm Vonni." With a nod of my head, I indicate the larger kid who stands frozen next to him. "Has this kid been bothering you for long?"

His dark eyes plead with me. "You won't k-kill him if I say, will y-you?"

"Go inside and find your dad." I glare at the larger boy, adding, "I'll be in shortly."

With a last look at his tormentor, he reluctantly takes off

down the alley.

"Do you know who I am?"

"You said your name is Vonni."

Even shaking, he tries to match my stare. His dark brown eyes glitter with repressed fury. The boy has balls, I'll give him that.

"It is. Vonni Moran."

Recognition dawns, and I can see the gears grinding inside his head, trying to figure out what this means for him. By the sour look on his face, I can tell he knows nothing good.

"Here's what's going to happen. You have just volunteered yourself to be young William's guardian angel. You will make sure that not a hair on his head is touched, even if you have to walk him here every day. If I find out William has had any problems, I'm coming for you personally." The boy doesn't need to know that shooting kids is against my code. "Do we understand each other?"

He looks from the gun to my face, nodding his head yes.

"Good. Now get out of here." As I holster my gun, the kid turns and begins walking back toward the street. I call out after him, "If I were you, I'd be here in the morning to walk William to school."

He says nothing, but I know he hears me by the stiffening of his shoulders. Luke is standing at the mouth of the alley watching the kid walk past him.

"Here you are." He looks between me and the kid's retreating form. "Everything all right?"

"Come on, let's grab some Chinese." I head toward The Golden Dragon, telling Luke, "I have a feeling this is the day Mr. Woo says yes."

TWENTY-FOUR

RACHAEL

When I pull out of the parking lot leaving work, I roll my windows down and turn my music up to clear my head. I'm lost in my jams as I arrive at the front of my apartment complex. Vonni, Sebastian, and Mandy get out of Vonni's SUV when they see me. With a smile, I wave as I get out of my Jeep.

"I see you have Vonni's shitty taste in music," Sebastian says with a smirk.

Mandy punches him in the stomach. "You'll have to forgive him. He likes metal or rock."

"I suppose a person has to have faults."

Sebastian's face scrunches up unattractively, making Vonni cough to cover up his laughter.

"I thought I'd ask them to tag along so you won't be bored while you're waiting for me."

"More so that I have protection than being bored while I'm waiting for you." I give Vonni the side eye. "Let me just run up and change."

"Wait here guys, I'll go up with Rachael," Mandy says,

walking up the steps behind me.

Shutting the door of my apartment behind us, I head down the hall toward my bedroom.

"Come back and help me with what to wear while you tell me whatever it is you're dying to tell me."

"What makes you think I have anything to say?"

When I turn around to look at her, she has a coy smile on her face.

"Oh, I don't know. You're hopping on one leg like you have to pee but haven't asked me where the bathroom is."

"I'm dying to tell someone, and you're the only person I can tell." She sits down on my hot pink and navy striped bedspread, patting the spot next to her. "Everyone else will freak."

"I love juicy gossip." I sit, turning to face her. "By the way, you look cute today."

Her pale pink tank top matches her pumps. Her darker pink skirt falls right above her knee, with tulle down the sides that remind me of a prima ballerina's tutu. A pink heart-shaped crystal hangs from a long silver chain.

"Thanks, girl." She crosses her legs and leans closer. "I'm no longer a virgin!"

Both her hands cover her mouth like she can't believe she just said that out loud.

"Shut the front door." I know my mouth is hanging open, but I can't seem to help it. "Sebastian is the first guy you've ever had sex with?"

"I mean, I've done other stuff with boyfriends, but it just never felt right before. Can I tell you something else?"

At my eager nod, she leans forward, looking around as if someone's going to jump out of my closet and eavesdrop. "Now I can't get enough. I've had sex twice today, and I'm already thinking about jumping him tonight."

"Since you shared, I'll share. It had been two years since the last time I'd had sex before Vonni. My friend Chantal unkindly pointed out that I was practically a virgin again.

There wasn't anyone that made me want to. I totally get what you're saying."

"Can I ask you a question?"

"Yes, but be kind."

"I heard about your ex-husband showing up at the docks. What happened that he's your ex?"

"He was cheating with multiple girls."

"I would have kicked him in the nuts when I saw him too."

Her earnest look, combined with the hand she puts on my arm in solidarity, makes me laugh so hard I've got tears streaming down my face.

"Mandy, we've got to hurry and get downstairs." I dab under my eyes as the last of my laughter dies. "The boys will think something happened to us."

"Let's do this," she says, a look of concentration on her face.

She peruses my closet, trying to decide as I stand next to her. I reach in, pulling out a fitted tank top dress in a neon green color. She nods in approval.

"I'll get to work on shoes and jewelry while you get changed."

The soft cotton of the dress feels good against my skin. Mandy hands me delicate gold heels, and a pair of large gold hoop earrings I forgot I had. Grabbing my purse off the bed, we head out.

Vonni holds the passenger door of the SUV open, watching me as I approach. He helps me in, letting his hand stay on my butt way longer than necessary.

"Where are we going for dinner?"

"There's a good steak place a block away from the club we're going to," he responds as he absentmindedly plays with my fingers as he drives.

"They have more than just steak," Mandy says from the back seat. "They also have a wonderful soup and salad bar."

I turn around to smile at her. "I love a soup and salad bar."

Vonni shakes his head. "We're going to a steak house, and

you're excited about a salad bar?"

The parking attendant stand sits in the middle of the restaurant's circular driveway. Sebastian and Mandy hold hands as they go inside ahead of us. Standing on the sidewalk, in front of a massive set of wooden doors, I wait for Vonni to give the parking attendant his key. He saunters up to me, grabbing my hand.

He leans in close, his breath hot against my ear as he whispers, "Are you wearing a thong?"

"You'll just have to find out for yourself," I say, running my hand along his cheek, loving the feel of his facial hair.

He opens the door of the restaurant, but when I enter the vestibule Mandy and Sebastian aren't anywhere to be seen.

"Follow me." A tall, willowy blonde ignores me completely to grin at Vonni. "I just sat the rest of your party."

Passing the hostess stand, we follow her down a dimly lit hallway. We make our way through a sea of tables until we reach Sebastian and Mandy tucked into an intimate booth at the back. A distinguished older gentleman with salt and pepper hair leans over as he talks to Mandy, tucking a red tie into his black suit.

Vonni lets go of my hand, stepping in front of me to shake hands with the gentleman. He turns back toward me, placing a hand on my hip to guide me forward.

"Rachael LaDeuc, this is Vito Cordone."

"Aww, I've heard about the lovely Rachael from John." He has a gleam in his eye that makes me uncomfortable. "Pleased to meet you."

"I'm pleased to meet you as well."

He extends his hand, and as soon as it touches mine, a shiver runs up my arm.

"I was just on my way out." He lets go of my hand and looks at Vonni. "I'll let you guys enjoy your meal."

"Take care, Vito."

Vonni slides into the booth after me, resting his hand on the top of my thigh. After Vito leaves, Mandy leans across the tabletop.

"Vito is the head of his family."

"Like John is the head of the Morans?"

"Yes. There are six families that run the city. It benefits everyone monetarily to work together."

Mandy leans back and grows silent as the server appears at our table. Despite Sebastian's stare of death, Mandy orders a margarita. The boys both order beer, and I opt for a glass of Pinot Grigio. For once, I'm sitting next to Vonni, so I'm not tempted to stare at the hand that drums on the tabletop.

"How was your first week at the docks?" Mandy asks, resting her hands under her chin.

"I give her a month with the dragon," Sebastian says.

Mandy swats him and looks at me.

"I don't know what you boys do to piss her off so much, but she's fine with me. I like to be busy, and she needs the help. She even cracked a joke about my reputation with the guys on the docks, even though I find the whole thing embarrassing."

"I heard all about it this morning," Sebastian says with a smirk.

"How long before the buzz dies down?"

"From what I heard, you dropped a big dude, walking away without a glance. That's not something the boys down at the docks see every day."

The server returns with our drinks and asks us for our dinner order. Everyone else orders steaks, while I get the soup and salad bar.

"You don't eat steak?" Vonni asks me after the server leaves. "We can go somewhere else."

"I love a soup and salad bar." I shrug. "Few places have one anymore."

I look across the booth, watching as Mandy whispers something in Sebastian's ear, Vonni's hand tightening on my thigh.

"I'm glad you let me set them up." I lean into him, whispering against his ear, "Mandy is thrilled."

He brushes his lips against my ear as he speaks, "Mandy's happiness is the only reason I haven't punched Seb in the face."

"You can't punch Sebastian because he fell for your sister. It's not something he planned."

He kisses my neck before whispering against my ear, "You seem kinda judgmental for a girl that threatened to cut his penis off and feed it to sharks."

Even though the touch of his lips is barely a brush, I still shudder.

"You've got me there."

Everyone eats in relative silence for a few minutes after the food arrives, before resuming idle conversation. Mandy and I head to the ladies' room while the guys pay the check.

"Vonni is taking Sebastian and I being together better than I could have hoped for." We stand next to each other in front of a row of mirrors, washing our hands. "I have you to thank for that."

"I would lie off the PDA for a while around Vonni for Sebastian's personal safety. I'm only one woman."

She laughs, holding the antique cream door open for me. "Noted."

She takes my advice on the walk over to the club, staying close to Sebastian, but not touching him. Vonni, on the other hand, runs his fingers up and down my back as we walk. Approaching a heavily muscled bouncer, Vonni rests his hand on my hip, keeping me close against his body. Sebastian comes up on my other side, with Mandy tucked under his arm.

"Vonni, Sebastian." The bouncer nods at each guy. "Who do you have with you?"

"Greg, this is my girl, Rachael. The girl with Sebastian is my sister, Mandy."

"Paul is waiting for you upstairs," Greg says, moving aside the red velvet rope.

Inclining his head, Vonni steers me through. The rap music that pumps from the speakers is loud enough that you have to lean in close to talk. He grabs my hand, leading me past a large center dance floor lined with tables. A bar runs along the entire right side of the building, ending at a set of stairs. The second floor has an open landing, with a DJ booth at the center. We pass several closed doors, presumably leading to either offices or private rooms, stopping at a small bar.

A petite brunette with shoulder length hair stands behind the bar. Leaning against the bar, Vonni waves his hand to get her attention. She comes toward him with a brilliant smile, lighting up her beautiful face. She runs her hand along his arm, leaning over the bar to the point her small yet perky boobs almost pop out of her tank top.

"Vonni, it's been too long," she says, with a pretty pout.

Gnashing my teeth together, I drive down the desire to grab her by her hair and bang her head against the bar.

"Kim, this is my girl, Rachael," Vonni says, disengaging himself from her grasp. "You already know Sebastian, but the girl with Sebastian is my sister, Mandy. While I'm in with Paul, get them whatever they want."

Lightly kissing me, he heads off toward the room closest to the bar, disappearing inside. She eyes me with a look of disappointment, to which I smirk.

"At least let me order a drink before you go across the bar," Sebastian whispers, poking me in the side.

"Well, get on with it then."

Sebastian looks hopefully in Mandy's direction after he orders his beer. "I don't suppose I can talk you into a soda?"

She laughs him off, ordering her signature margarita.

"Please give me whatever your favorite drink to make is."

"Nobody ever says that. I have something I've been working on that I'd like you to try."

She pours what appears to be small amounts of several bottles of alcohol, adding several juices. Shaking the concoction, she pours it into a long-stemmed glass before handing it to me.

"Kim, this is excellent," I tell her after taking a sip. "What do you call it?"

"I'm still working on a name, but for now we'll call it the Kim special," she says with a bright smile plastered across her face.

"I'll be back for another if this one doesn't set me on my ass."

Even with the music, I hear her laughter well after we move away from the bar.

"Look at you." Sebastian looks at me, smiling, "Being all adult and making friends."

Mandy stands next to him, giggling behind her hand.

"Ever heard the expression keep your friends close, and your enemies closer?"

We sit at one grouping of red velvet couches, watching the people on the dance floor below. After several songs, Mandy stands up, taking my hand.

"Come on, let's dance. I didn't come to sit and watch."

Laughing, I let her lead me down the stairs and onto the dance floor. Sebastian stands by the long bar, sipping his beer as he watches us. It had been too long since the last time I danced, and I quickly lose myself in the music.

"You want to get another drink?" Mandy leans in to ask, after dancing for quite some time.

Nodding my head yes, I hold her hand, following her to where Sebastian's leaning against the bar. He signals the bartender, ordering us both a margarita. We watch the crowd while sipping our drinks.

Sebastian leans in so we can both hear him. "I gotta hit the head, I'll be right back." He gives us a stern look, pointing at both of us. "Don't go anywhere."

Mandy rolls her eyes at Sebastian behind his back. When she faces me again, her dark blue eyes get as big as saucers. I turn around to see what she's staring at, only to come face to chest with a thin man with dark hair. He stands extremely close, leering down at me.

"How about a dance?"

He leans in even closer, running his finger down my arm.

"No, thanks." I eye his finger. "I'm dancing with my girlfriend."

"Come on. What's one dance?"

Only a few feet away on the left, I see Sebastian working his way toward us, but it's Vonni's voice I hear behind me.

"Take a fucking walk."

The guy ignores him and turns back to me. Quick as lightning, Vonni moves, punching him in the jaw. The guy crumbles to the floor, not moving.

"Was that necessary?"

He doesn't say a word to me. Instead, he reaches into his pocket and hands Sebastian the valet slip.

"Get them outta here, I'll catch up."

Sebastian grabs both of our arms, steering us out of the club. When we hit the sidewalk, he takes out his phone.

"Where are you at?" Then a pause. "Good. Bring them with you, and head over to Paul's right away for damage control. I had to leave Vonni by himself to get Rachael and Mandy home."

After another pause, he hangs up. On the walk back to the restaurant, I stew in silence. Mandy turns to Sebastian at the valet stand while we're waiting for him to bring our car around.

"Who's going to meet Vonni?"

"Luke was around the corner playing pool with Johnny and DJ, so they'll get to him in no time."

As the SUV drives up, she nods. Sebastian gets into the driver's seat with Mandy in the passenger's seat and me in the back. I'm not sure how many times Mandy tries to talk to me while I'm staring out the window sulking. She finally catches my attention by turning to face the back seat.

"What are you mad about?"

"If he plans on punching every guy that hits on me, he's going to pay out a lot of lawsuits."

"Of all my brothers, he's the most levelheaded. Ive' never seen him punch a guy for hitting on the woman he's with before."

"He gave the guy a warning." Sebastian looks at me in the rearview mirror. "He told him to take a fucking walk. Dude didn't listen. Bet he wishes he did now. I've never seen a Moran that couldn't throw a punch. They can take a punch too."

Sebastian pulls up to the curb, getting out to walk me to the front door. "Call Mandy when you get into your apartment."

"Thanks, Sebastian."

Heading up the stairs, I let myself into my apartment. After locking the door behind me, I dig my phone out to call Mandy.

"Hey, I'm in. You guys can take off. Have fun, you two."

I'm still pissed at Vonni, but there's something else bothering me, though. I'm not sure what's got under my skin. Maybe a nice soak in the tub with a cup of hot tea will help me work it out. Laying back in my bubble bath, I wrap my hands around my mug and sip my tea. The uncomfortable feeling in my chest persists. When I close my eyes, it hits me. I know what I must do. A quick trip to the reservation is in order.

TWENTY-FIVE

VONNI

When Rachael asked me if punching the guy was necessary, I knew she was mad. She wouldn't have liked my answer either. Fuck yeah, it was necessary. The prick's lucky that's all he got was coldcocked.

First strike was making the mistake of laying a hand on my girl. Nobody touches her but me. Second strike was harassing her. His refusing to take no for an answer, repeatedly, pissed me off. Third strike was failing to heed the warning I gave him. Ordinarily I wouldn't have given the dude a warning, but causing Paul problems is bad for business.

"What the fuck happened, Vonni?" Paul waves his hand at the still prone form of the guy who messed with Rachael lying on the red leather couch in his office. "Greg had to carry him up here."

"He made the mistake of touching what's mine." I meet his gaze and lean forward. "I'll clean up my mess. If you require compensation for your trouble, that won't be a problem."

It's all I can think of to make the situation right with Paul.

He sits behind his desk with his hands threaded together. Three quick knuckle pounds come from the other side of the door before Greg pokes his head around the door's frame.

"Boss, Luke, Johnny, and DJ are here for Vonni."

"Send them in," he tells him, motioning with his fingers.

Sebastian must have placed a call after he left to take the girls home. Paul isn't in the Mafia, but he's every bit as dangerous. In our circles he's known for being a provider of weapons or information, not that he shies away from taking the occasional job as a hit man. Never taking my eyes off him, I can feel my family standing behind my chair. Paul's eyes roam between the four of us.

"Leave out the back way." He stands. "Take your trash with you, and I'll consider us even."

Standing, I reach across the desk to shake his hand. Everyone else springs into action with DJ grabbing one side and Johnny the other, while Luke gets the back door of Paul's office.

The door opens into the back alley of the club. When the door swings shut behind us, Luke looks at me.

"What happened back there? Sebastian said to get over to Paul's right away. He had to leave you behind to take the girls home."

"When I came out of my meeting with Paul, I caught this guy giving Rachael a hard time."

"Well, you got him good." DJ shakes his head. "He's dead weight."

"How do you want to handle this?"

Johnny inclines his head toward the guy before grunting and adjusting positions.

There's a groan before the guy opens his eyes, looking around. His gaze snaps to me, the sudden *O* forming on his lips is priceless.

"Set him down, guys."

DJ sets his feet down while Johnny helps him to stand, keeping a hand on him until he's steady.

"How did I get to the alleyway?" he asks, rubbing his jaw and looking between the four of us.

"You've been out awhile, dude." Luke laughs. "Think you can drive home?"

"That was a heck of a punch." He meets my gaze. "Not sure if I want to sue you or if I should be impressed."

"Asshole, you're lucky he didn't kill you," DJ speaks up, indicating me with his thumb. "You were hitting on Vonni Moran's girl."

While his look of horror is almost as satisfying as punching him, what I really want to be doing is sliding into bed beside Rachael.

"I wouldn't recommend suing, considering my lawyers are better than yours. How about you consider yourself lucky all you got was a punch." I reach into my breast pocket and pull out a large wad of bills, handing it to him. "Take this and forget you were ever here before I change my mind."

TWENTY-SIX

RACHAEL

Vonni lies sprawled out next to me, breathing deeply, and I reach over, running my hand through his hair. With a sigh, I get up, careful not to wake him as I dress. Leaving him a note on my pillow, I stand there with my backpack slung over my shoulder, gazing down at his beautiful features. His firm jaw sprinkled with the perfect amount of facial hair, and ridiculously long lashes fanning against his smooth skin. My heart lurches in my chest as I walk away.

There are only sanitation workers out at this hour, so I make good time leaving the city. Rolling down my windows, I feel the wind bite my cheeks. The morning chill dissipates as I crank up my favorite song. An hour outside the reservation, my phone rings.

"Good morning," I answer, expecting Vonni's call.

"I woke up to a note telling me you've gone to the reservation, and you'd be back tomorrow morning. Is reservation a code for something?"

"It's not a code." I laugh. "My grandmother is Native

American, and lives on the reservation."

He's silent for a moment. "Cara, you're running away."

Being in love with someone who both understands and challenges me is a novel experience. I'm close with all my family, but my grandmother is the only one who calls me on my baggage. It's why I'm running to her now. Is it possible I'm wrong to think she will be the only one to understand my mixed-up emotions over Vonni? Maybe Vonni himself understands me just as well as she does. The silence stretches as I chew on my lip, lost in my feelings.

"I know you're mad at me over what happened at the club. It pissed me off the way he looked at you. Then he fucking put his hands on you." He pauses. "I can't tell you it will never happen again, because that would be a lie."

"I fantasized about smashing Kim's head against the bar when she was busy rubbing your arm and showing you her breasts. However, she's very much unharmed. It's going to be a long road if you plan on punching any guy who hits on me."

"Is it terrible that I love you being jealous?"

"I think you are missing the point."

"Will you come back now if I promise I will try to do better?" he asks, sounding equal parts resigned and pained.

"I'm going to hold you to that. I have something I need to do before I come back. Just give me a day."

"I'm not known for being patient." He heaves a sigh. "If you take too long, I will come after you."

He hangs up and I try not to be put out by the thought of Vonni coming after me, but a small part of me is aching with the image of him doing just that. It makes me squirm in my seat, but that's why I need my grandmother, because my next instinct is to bury my head in the sand and hide.

The land on the outskirts of the reservation has a natural beauty that always brings me peace. Driving through the gates, I pass a handful of businesses that help to keep the reservation self-sufficient. A small mom and pop grocery store, gas station, and post office.

This entire section of the reservation reminds me of an old west movie set. I pass a row of brick front clothing stores before pulling in front of the only jewelry store. There are wood slats that look like they belong on an old roof instead of a storefront. Jewelry isn't the only thing they sell. The few tourists that come onto the reservation love this place because they have things like wood carvings and dream catchers.

When Sally catches sight of me, she comes around from behind the counter to hug me. We stand there, holding each other for a moment before she pushes me away. Her raven hair bobs around her face. Her chocolate eyes framed by her tortoiseshell glasses bore into me.

"I thought once you moved to the city we wouldn't see you for a long time."

"You can't get rid of me that easy. You know I love your dad's store."

"Has your grandmother seen you yet?" a booming voice asks from behind me.

Turning to look at Alo, I smile. His raven hair is shot through with gray. It's in a braid that falls over one shoulder.

"No, you are my first stop on the way in."

"Good," he says with a broad grin. "I can needle her about it when we play cards tonight."

"She'll allow you anything."

"Now let's get down to business." He crosses his arms over his barrel chest. "What can I help you with?"

"I have something in mind I want to buy, and you're the only one I know that might have it. I'm looking for a man's silver ring, about the size and thickness of a class ring. Instead of a stone at the center, it has the head of a wolf."

He taps his chin, thinking for a moment. "Come with me. I think I have just the thing."

Following him to the back of the store, I watch as he walks behind a clear glass jewelry counter. He runs his hand along the top of the glass as he looks. Stopping near the end, he takes out a ring, holding it up for me to see.

"It's perfect." In his hand is a replica of what I saw in my mind last night. "What size is it?"

"I have two rings. One is a size ten and one is an eleven. I can solder either down or up by two sizes."

"No soldering necessary. The ten looks like it will fit."

He takes out a ring box from behind him and sets the ring inside. Carrying the box, he heads to the register where Sally is sitting on a wooden stool.

"A man's ring, huh," Sally comments after looking in the box.

"It's a present for a special guy."

"Does your grandmother know about this special guy?" Alo asks, leaning against the pine countertop.

"You get to brag to her you heard about him first. I'm on my way to talk to her."

I drive farther into the reservation where businesses drop off and the residential section starts. Some people who live on the reservation occupy small brick six-unit apartments, while others live in either single or double wide trailers. My grandmother's trailer is the very last one on the right. Its pale yellow color is bright and cheerful.

She's sitting on her porch in her old wooden rocking chair. As soon as she sees me get out of the Jeep, she stands up, smiling.

"I thought I might see you today."

My grandmother has second sight, or the ability to see things before they happen. When I was ten, I told her I wished I had inherited her ability. With a sad look on her face, she told me she was glad that I hadn't.

It wasn't until my parents died in a car accident a few years later that I understood what she meant. She's never gotten over seeing that vision and being aware that she was too late to do anything about it. Now that I think about it, that must be why she was so upset about the wolf's vision.

Her long graying hair is pulled back into her customary

bun. Her tan skin still holds a youthful glow despite her advancing age, and her brown eyes are still as warm and wise as they always are.

"You look good," I say, smiling up at her from the bottom step. "I just came from seeing Alo."

"What will the old coot be bragging about tonight?"

Her words might have been harsh, but her affection is clear. She and Alo grew up together, but she left the reservation as a teenager in search of adventure. Instead, she found my grandfather. They had a passionate marriage until his death ten years ago. She told me she knew it was her destiny to return to her roots. In doing so, she had also returned to Alo.

"I went by his store on my way in and bought a man's ring."

Looking up at her, I try to gauge her reaction.

"My vision has to come to pass." Her brow crinkles. "Your wolf has found you. Do you love him?"

"Yes, and I'm an absolute mess because of it."

"Come inside and we'll talk."

We stand facing each other in her kitchen. Her collection of roosters are crammed in all the spots she might fit them in. I'm pretty sure she has a rooster for anything kitchen related.

"I know it's a little early, but you might need this."

She pours two shots from a rum bottle, sliding mine across the counter. We both drink the shot. It burns in my chest, and I know I'm ready to talk.

"Now all we have to do is figure out how to keep your wolf safe."

"I'm going to take his ring to the shaman before I give it to him."

"Who says you don't have second sight?" She smiles. "You bought him a wolf ring."

"If you knew who this man was, you would know a threat isn't out of the way. It has nothing to do with sight."

At least I don't think so, I've never asked my grandmother

how her gift works.

"Is that what holds you back?"

Sinking down to sit on her kitchen floor, I put my head in my hands and sob. She bends over, placing her hand on my head, her fingers stroking through my hair. For long moments, we remain like that until my tears dry up.

"Grandmother, I'm scared. Loving him will take all I have."

"That is always the case. If it is not, then it will not last. I told you not to marry Dan, but you wouldn't listen. No matter how far you go, you can't outrun love, my darling. Pull yourself together and go to the shaman. Get the blessing you need."

Slowly, I stand up, hugging her hard before I set out. The shaman of the tribe adheres to the traditional practices of our culture, and if you want his blessing, you do as well. That means you can't drive to reach his hut, but it's not an arduous walk from my grandmother's trailer either.

There's a trail you can follow through the woods, and if you keep a brisk pace, it's only about an hour's walk. Since starting my new job and meeting Vonni, I haven't been working out. It feels good to exercise my muscles in the comfort of nature. The temperature is a balmy seventy degrees and I'm breaking into a light sweat, but I don't mind. I listen to nature's creatures sing and scurry, moving through the canopy, with the bright sun illuminating my way.

The shaman's hut is traditional in that it's made from wood and thatch, with smoke and incense escaping through the roof. Lifting the flap, I enter. A beautifully made carpet partially covers hard packed dirt floors. The shaman sits cross-legged on a pile of pillows with his eyes closed. He opens one eye, indicating the pile of pillows across from him.

"What can I do for you today, Rachael?"

He's always direct and approaches everything with businesslike efficiency, even though what he does for the tribe has nothing to do with business.

Sitting cross-legged, I dig the ring out of my backpack,

laying it before him. "I need your blessing. The owner of the ring will need protection."

"A wolf," he says, picking up the ring and studying it.

"It reminds me of him. A dangerous predator, to be sure, but fiercely loyal and protective of his pack."

He waves the incense around the ring, closing his eyes and crooning. Closing my eyes, I reach out with my senses. In my mind, I see the wolf from my grandmother's vision as he runs. When he reaches the edge of the forest, the wolf morphs into Vonni. Overwhelming fear grips me. Suddenly, what I see in my mind's eye changes, and I'm back in the shaman's hut. When I open my eyes, I find him watching me.

"When the time comes, do not hesitate, or all will be lost to you," he says, handing me back the ring.

After placing the ring back in my book bag, I open another compartment and get out my wallet, fishing out some bills. "I know you don't normally accept payment in this currency, but it's all I can offer. You've given me something of value. To let you go empty-handed doesn't sit right."

"Rachael, I accept any currency offered." His dark hair falls forward, brushing against his naked chest as he takes the money. "It's just payment usually comes in other ways."

Rising, I breathe in deeply before thanking him. How he knows the things he does is a mystery to pretty much everyone. It doesn't change the fact he's never wrong, just like my grandmother.

When I return to my grandmother's trailer, I don't see her on the porch. When I enter without knocking, I find her in the kitchen making sandwiches.

"You always make the best tuna salad," I tell her, leaning against the countertop.

"Sit." She indicates the short wooden stool with her spoon. "I'm just finishing up and we'll have lunch. Kevin said Nancy told Dan where you worked." She eyes me. "He was worried about him showing up. Did he?"

"He tried to talk to me in the parking lot. I didn't have time for his nonsense, so I kicked him in the nuts. It's all the guys on the docks can talk about, much to my embarrassment."

She chuckles. "That's my girl."

I clean up the kitchen and meet my grandmother on the porch. As I sit down, my grandmother's dog makes an appearance. Her German Shepherd, Sergeant, has the run of the reservation. He comes up, butting me in the hand for me to pet him. His cat isn't far behind. Tibbs wandered in with Sergeant one day, and just never left. Where you see Sergeant, Tibbs isn't far behind. Tibbs jumps up onto my lap, purring, until I pet him with my other hand.

We sit on the porch until early evening when Alo and Sally come back from working at the store carrying a pizza. Alo has a serious demeanor, but he always lights up when he first sees my grandmother. Sally and I look at each other and roll our eyes.

There's a brief knock on the door right as we finish eating and my cousins Kevin and Bobby barge in without waiting for anyone to answer the door.

"Look what the cat dragged in," I say, the sight of them making me smile.

Kevin envelopes me in a bear hug. "You didn't think you'd sneak into town without seeing us, did you?"

"We've come to steal you," Bobby says, leaning in to kiss my cheek. "There's a pool hall slash bar now on the reservation."

"We are moving up in the world." I turn to Sally. "Are you coming with us?"

"I wouldn't miss it."

Sally's our favorite designated driver since she never touches alcohol, anyway. It turns out the new bar isn't far from my grandmother's trailer. From the outside, it looks like a large wooden country farmhouse, complete with rocking chairs.

When we walk in the door, a dart flies past us, coming to land in the center of the board that hangs to the left of the door. We move out of the way of danger, walking past the pool tables on the way to the bar. The girl behind the bar looks familiar, but I can't quite place her. She has a stylish bob that's dyed a dark blue color. She looks up from pouring a beer and it hits me. It's Megan from high school. There's no mistaking her startling green eyes. She sets the beer down, coming around on the side by the jukebox.

"I thought that was you." She envelopes me in a big hug. "I heard you moved to the city, what are you doing here?"

"I did. It's a quick trip, I head back tomorrow."

She goes back behind the bar. "What are you guys having?"

The boys both get beer, Sally her standard Coke, and I get a glass of wine. We sit at the bar talking with Megan until the place fills up, and she gets too busy to keep up a conversation. Bobby moves over to one of the pool tables and begins setting up.

"Don't make a big deal about it, but Bobby and Sally are an item," Kevin whispers in my ear. "They try to hide it, but you'll see."

"Get out. What about you?"

The set of his mouth and the look in his dark eyes scream "don't ask."

"You ever think about Kendra?"

"You know better than to be in my business about girls." He scowls, his mustache looking comically lopsided. "Just out of curiosity, has she said anything about me?"

"She referred to you as a handsome devil and asked what you were up to."

Sinking my shot, I give him a sly grin.

With a wary look, he misses his shot. "What did you say?"

"Same old." I shoot one of his striped balls into my solid, sinking it. "She heard about you working at the plant."

"Did she?"

He leans over, lining up his shot.

"I think she remembers you fondly." He rubs his hand over

the back of his neck, a sure sign of his discomfort. "You should call her sometime."

He drags a hand through his short, dark hair. "If you shut up about it, maybe I will."

"Whatever."

I shrug, taking my last shot. It rolls to the corner slowly before falling in.

"Damn. I was hoping your game had gone to shit. I'll be right back."

"What was that all about?" Bobby asks, pointing at Kevin's retreating form.

"A girl that he evidently still has a thing for. He screwed it up a little, but I have a feeling she may forgive him."

"Don't we all screw it up sometimes and hope like hell the other person forgives us?"

"In the LaDeuc clan anyway, that's true."

Bobby asks, "Are you back here to see your grandma because you screwed it up?"

"Not screwed it up, more like running scared," I admit, chewing my lower lip.

"I feel you."

He takes a swig of his beer, watching Sally at the bar.

"Is she the one who has you running scared?"

I follow his gaze, nodding toward Sally.

"Huh, what are you talking about?"

He tries to play cool, but his gray eyes watch every move she makes.

"You don't have to pretend, the gig is up. Sally is a brilliant girl. If I were you, I wouldn't hide a thing."

His grimace is partially hidden by his full dark beard. "You don't have to face Alo."

Dan looms in front of me, like the Loch Ness Monster that's suddenly making a shadow under your canoe. How does he keep finding me? Sneaking up on me is more like it.

"Can I talk to you a minute?" Dan asks, covering his crotch with both hands.

Bobby moves in front of me to stand toe-to-toe with Dan. Well, as close as Bobby can get. He's only about five foot eight, whereas Dan's well over six foot three. Dan is a solid wall of muscle whereas Bobby's trim.

"Bobby, I'll be fine," I say, putting a hand on his arm. "Can you give us a minute?"

"I'll go talk to Sally at the bar." He turns to Dan. "I'll be watching you."

He bumps into him hard before walking away.

"How did you know I was here?"

His recent habit of instantaneously showing up where I am is freaking me out.

"Chris saw you leaving Alo's place earlier today and called me. I took a chance your cousins would bring you here tonight. If I didn't catch you tonight, I was going to stop by your grandma's in the morning."

"Well, you found me." I cross my arms over my chest and give him my best death stare. "You sure have gone to a lot of trouble to track me down."

"Listen, I shouldn't have grabbed you the other day. Obviously, that was the wrong thing to do." He readjusts himself. "I've started seeing someone, professionally that is."

"Wow, that's a big step." While we were together, he would never seek professional help for childhood trauma he suffered at the hands of his mother. No matter how many times I brought it up. "I'm thrilled for you."

"She says I need closure, or some shit. Here goes nothing. I fucked it all up. It had nothing to do with you, or anything you did. I was struggling with my depression again, and the attention of other women made me feel good. For a little while, anyway. I never meant to hurt you, hell I never even meant for you to find out. I know we can't go back, but I hope in time you can forgive me."

"I forgave you a long time ago, but I'm glad you told me what you did. You made me wonder for a long time if I just wasn't any good in bed." Dan won't be following me anymore, and I feel a deep sense of relief. "I'm sorry, too, for kicking you in the nuts."

"No shit." He puts a hand in front of his private parts and bends down. "Don't kick me in the nuts for this. You gave the best head I've ever had."

I place my hand in front of my face, trying to smother a giggle.

Kevin approaches us cautiously and says, "There's something I thought I'd never see. Are you ok, Rachael?"

"I'm just fine."

"Take care, Rachael," Dan says before he turns and walks out the door without a backward glance.

Bobby looks back and forth between Kevin and me. "Are you guys ready to go?"

"Yeah, I am."

Kevin holds the door of the bar open for me. "What the hell was that?"

"That was Dan being an adult and owning his behavior." I open my door and get in. "He apologized."

"You guys good now?" Sally asks, backing out of the parking space.

I look out the window and say, "I guess we are."

TWENTY-SEVEN

VONNI

I'm not sure what to do when I hang up with Rachael. Evidently, she didn't learn her lesson the first time she tried to run, only to come home and find me in her bed. Instead, she ran farther this time. I have no intention of letting it continue. When she's upset with me, I need her to stay and deal with it, no matter what it is. That's asking a lot of her, considering who I am.

My first instinct is to handcuff her to the bed until I get my way. While that idea has definite merit, ultimately it won't get me what I want long-term. Neither, unfortunately, will it benefit me to go after her too soon. She asked me for one day, but today is all she's going to get. After that, I have no intention of letting Rachael spend even one night outside of my bed. That's when a plan takes shape in my mind.

I sigh, looking down at my phone. There's one person I need on my side for my plan to work. Favors are something people owe me, not the other way around. He owes me one and now is the time to collect.

Kevin picks up on the first ring. "Vonni Moran. It's been a while. Since you're calling me out of the blue, this can't be good. Just so we're clear, I'm still a terrible shot."

"Yeah, it's been about a year since you left." I chuckle. "I haven't forgotten about the time you and Christian got drunk, and Christian thought it would be a good idea to give you his gun. Damn near winged Rafe."

I pause. "Unfortunately, I'm calling because I need a favor. I need to know how to get to Rachael's grandmother's house."

"We both know I owe you one for saving my ass when I hit on the wrong man's wife." Kevin's voice takes on a hard edge. "What I don't know is what my cousin has to do with anything."

Kevin is by nature suspicious and protective. Normally, I admire those things about him. Today, however, it's frustrating as hell. If I had more than a day to play with, I could have just called Rafe and saved myself the trouble of answering his questions.

"With or without your help, I plan to bring her back home with me tomorrow morning." He doesn't need to know that I'm not sure if I can make that happen without his help. "She asked me for a day, and that's what I'm giving her."

"Fuck, why would she bother to listen to me now when she never has? I should have known telling her to stay away from the Morans was going to have the opposite effect. To think Christian was the one I was worried about."

"To be fair, we were already involved when you told her that."

"Does she know?"

I couldn't pretend I didn't know exactly what he was asking.

"Yes," I say between clenched teeth. "The fact that I'm letting you question me at all should tell you something. She is mine. You know better than anyone the penalty for messing with what's mine. I've always liked you, but nobody stands in the way of what I want."

"Do you have a pad and a pen?"

TWENTY-EIGHT

RACHAEL

Light is streaming in the window when I open my eyes. Stretching, I head to the shower, feeling too gross to even approach small talk at the moment. Under the hot spray of water, I quickly scrub. I'm eager to see Vonni, even though I've only been away from him for a day.

When I leave the steam of the bathroom behind, the trailer is still and silent. The coffeepot is on, and fresh fruit sits in a bowl on the counter. I grab both, heading out to the porch. My grandmother is already there with a cup of coffee in her hand. This morning she's missing her customary bun, instead leaving her hair to trail down her back. Her feet rest on the railing, crossed at the ankles.

"You were tired, so I let you be," she says, turning to flash her dimples at me.

"Thanks, I needed it. I have to get going soon, though, it's already after ten."

"Are you stopping at your usual spot on the way out of town?" she asks, her dark eyes glittering with affection.

"You're the one with second sight, you tell me."

I shoot her a sideways glance, trying not to laugh.

"You always had a smart mouth like your grandfather," she huffs.

"You're the one who married him."

She has a faraway look on her face. "He was debonair and wooed me by whispering naughty things in French in my ear."

"I'm scandalized."

I put a hand to my chest, pretending to swoon.

"You better get back to your man." She waves me off with a flick of her slender wrist. "Haven't sat still since you've been out here."

Kissing her cheek, I go inside to wash my dishes. After making sure I have everything, I throw my backpack over my shoulder. Even though I'm only five foot four, I still have to bend over to hug her long and hard before I get into the car.

A river runs through the middle of the small town just outside the reservation. There are cute bridges with old stone parapets that border them. In some places it's so narrow you can throw a stone across, while in other places it's so wide you have to take a ferry to reach the other side.

On the back side of the statue, there are two gravel parking places. Getting out of the car, I reach for my backpack. The front side of the statue faces the river, and I sit in my customary spot in the middle of the base.

My eyes follow the water to the right, watching it wind around to another statue. This one is almost identical to the Washington Monument, except it's on a significantly smaller scale, and you can't enter it. The town uses the sprawling lawn that leads from the monument to the river as outdoor venue space. It's quite beautiful in the summer when fireworks light the night sky. Beyond that, I can just make out an old stone bridge. To my left, I watch the river widen. There are only trees and water for as far as I can see in that direction.

With my back against the statue, I take in the scenery. From behind me, I hear the crunch of tires on gravel. People park here to walk along the river. There's a long sidewalk that goes over the bridge into town in one direction, or toward a pretty residential section in the other. A shadow falls across me.

"You're a hard lady to find."

Vonni sits next to me, his shoulder brushing against mine. When I turn to drink in the sight of his face, I notice dark purple circles under his eyes.

"Vonni, are you ok?"

"Yeah, why?"

I reach out my hand, running my fingers under both of his eyes.

"I didn't sleep well at my place." He frowns. "In between tossing and turning, I had bizarre dreams that I was a wolf. I've been up since three."

"Were you running through the forest after your mate?"

"Now that's creepy, how did you know that?"

"Well, in order to tell you that, I have to give you a gift." I'm not really surprised he tracked me down, he warned me that he would. "First, though, how did you find me?"

"I called your cousin Kevin to find out how to get to your grandmother's. This morning when I pulled up, she was sitting on the porch. When I went to introduce myself, she said I was late and if I didn't hurry, I'd miss you. After she gave me directions, she kissed me on the forehead. I thought maybe she'd lost all her marbles, but what the hell, I drove this far, I could go see a statue. It shocked me when I pulled up and saw your Jeep."

A strange look crosses his features. "I'm sorry. I'm having a really weird morning. Did you say you got me a gift?"

"My grandmother isn't losing it." I laugh. "She's gifted with the ability to see things before they happen sometimes. We call it second sight. She must have seen you coming and wasn't sure how long I would sit here for. Why would Kevin tell you where I was, after telling me to stay away from the Morans?"

166

"Let's just say he owed me one." His mouth quirks to one side. "Now my gift. I've never had a woman buy me a gift before. Well, unless she was related to me."

"Really, none of the women you dated ever bought you anything? Not even a Christmas present? Let's also back up to exactly how Kevin owes you one."

"My previous relationships with women were more arrangements of convenience." He pauses, staring at his hands. "As for Kevin, all I'll say is he found himself in a situation that I could clear up on his behalf. If you want to know more, you'll have to ask him."

"Oh, I will definitely ask him."

He meets my gaze, the smirk on his lips widening. "I don't doubt that for a second, cara."

"Have you ever heard any of the legends of my tribe?" He shakes his head no. "Centuries ago, the gods blessed our tribe with the ability to change into a wolf."

He puts up his hand to stop me, his eyebrow about in his hairline. "Like werewolves?"

"Not quite. The term werewolf implies your change is tied into the phases of the moon and thus can't be helped. This was more like being a shapeshifter. You could become the wolf whenever you desired, for as long as you desired."

"Anyway, the tribe prospered using the wolf's abilities. One day, they grew greedy, killing solely for the thrill of the chase. The gods became angry. As punishment, we were doomed to remain human, with the soul of the beast trapped within. Wolves, to this day, are revered among the tribe. You are fortunate to see a wolf in the forest. They're a reminder of what once was."

Taking the box from my backpack, I hand it to him. "The wolf may be a dangerous predator, but it's also a loyal protector."

He eagerly opens the box, taking the ring out and studying it. "The detail on the wolf is amazing, considering the whole thing is made from silver. It's quite beautiful." He looks at me and smiles. "Aren't the guys supposed to buy the rings?"

"Normally, yes, but your ring is special. While the shaman was blessing it with protection, I saw a beautiful chestnut wolf with eyes the exact shade of blue as yours. I think my vision and your dream go together."

"Then I will never take it off."

He slides it onto his ring finger. A perfect fit. He watches me for a moment before he leans in to kiss me. The kiss begins as the lightest brush of his lips against mine. Bringing his hand to my jaw, he tilts my head to the exact spot he wants it. He runs his tongue along the part of my lips. To get his attention, I pull on the hair at the nape of his neck, breaking the kiss.

"I told you I was coming back today, why did you come all this way to find me?"

"After we hung up yesterday, I thought you needed a tangible reminder of me to keep you from running away when things get hard."

He strokes along my jaw as he speaks. "I can't promise you it won't be difficult, but I can promise you will never doubt my loyalty or my love." When my mouth falls open, he smirks. "You can't be shocked. I knew you loved me the day you cried all over me in your kitchen because you thought I was dead."

"You're very smug."

His eyes grow dark, his tone serious. "Tell me anyway, cara."

"I'm in love with you, Vonni."

My gaze travels from his eyes to his lips and back up.

He showers small kisses across my face. "I want to hear it again."

"I love you, Von."

He continues pressing featherlight kisses along my jaw. Taking my left hand in his, he slides a ring onto my finger. When I look down at my hand, I see a large rectangular emerald sitting atop a delicate silver band. My eyes snap from the ring to his handsome face.

"Vonni, it's so beautiful."

"I want you to be mine in every way." His face is more serious than I have ever seen it, and that's saying something. "Marry me, cara."

Tears fall down my cheeks. He watches me, using his thumbs to wipe away my tears. "What's wrong, cara?"

"They're happy tears, Vonni."

"You still haven't answered me," he says, his brows lifting.

"I can't have a minute to shed some ugly tears around you, can I?" His brows furrow and I smile. "Yes, Vonni, I will marry you." He crushes me against his body, kissing along my neck. My hand runs along his jaw until he meets my eyes. "I am curious. Why an emerald instead of a diamond?"

"Aside from it being my favorite color, emeralds are rare, like you, cara."

I thread my hands through his hair, kissing him with all the pent-up emotion I feel for him in that moment. My heart beats faster in my chest as he draws me across his lap, rubbing my thigh with his hand. Tipping me so my hip rests against his erection, his hand comes up to message my butt. My hands run down his chest, feeling the wild beating of his heart under my palm. With my palm, I push against his chest, speaking against his lips.

"Vonni, can we go home and continue this somewhere softer and less public?"

"I wish. Mandy blabbed about me buying a ring, so I have been ordered to bring you to my parents' house when we get back. I may have been stewing over my revenge on the way up here."

"That's rather sweet, if you ask me. There's only one problem, I can't go to your mom's house in yoga pants and a T-shirt."

"Sweet, ha. You're not the one having to walk around your parents' house with a hard-on. I wasn't planning to take no for an answer. I packed a dress and shoes for you to change into."

"Did you notice the historical house across the street from

the small parking lot?"

My breath fans along his neck as I wait for his reply.

"I can't say I paid any attention," he says, his voice guttural and his accent thick.

"The curator leaves between eleven and one for lunch every day." I suck on his earlobe a second before I continue. "They leave the place unlocked so I can change into my dress there." I trail my hand down his stomach to his erection and rub my palm against it. "I might need help to get undressed."

TWENTY-NINE

VONNI

My cock is painfully hard, even though I'm sitting on cold stone. It has always been that way with her. Hell, even being near her makes my dick twitch. She stands, throwing her backpack over her shoulder. With one of her sexy smiles, she holds out her hand. Grabbing it, I stand and follow behind her. Lord, her ass is a thing of beauty in those tight-fitting pants and thinking about the way her ass overflows my hands makes me decide to fuck her from behind.

"Don't forget my clothes," she says, turning around.

She gives me a wink, and I damn near pass my SUV. Opening the back door, I reach in to grab her dress and shoes. When I shut the car door, she stands there with her finger crooked, beckoning me to follow her. She doesn't look back as she crosses the street, heading toward a small white house with black shutters.

She holds the door open and stands just inside a small living room with antique furniture. After she shuts the door behind us, she takes my hand and leads me into a connecting room that's identical in size. A piano stands at the center of the room. The thought of bending her over it makes me stop next to the bench, and she has to pull on my hand to get me to follow. The only reason I do is I'm curious about what she has in mind.

She leads me into a small office off the kitchen at the back of the house. The only furniture in the room is an old rolltop desk with a wooden chair. She turns a gold skeleton key in the lock. It's sexy as hell that my girl is freaky enough to let me fuck her in an old historic house, but modest enough to pick a room with a locking door. Setting her shoes and dress on the desk, I pull out the chair, turning it toward her.

"Take off your clothes and hand them to me."

Absentmindedly, I throw the clothes on the desk as she hands them to me. There is nothing I like better than letting my eyes wander over her naked body. She runs her hands along my chest before undoing the buttons on my dress shirt, starting with the neck. She's only a few buttons in when I grow impatient, and moving her hands aside, I pull my shirt over my head and throw it on the desk.

She stands there staring at the bulge in my jeans. I love the intensity of her gaze as she watches me unzip and unbutton them. Before I release my cock, I rub my hand along my length through my jeans. Her quick intake of breath as she waits makes me want her even more. I pull off both my jeans and boxers and stand there for a minute. She reaches for my cock, but I grab her hand. If she touches me now, I'll never last, and there's still too much I want to do to her.

"Turn around and put your right leg on the chair."

I love that even though she doesn't know what I'm going to do, she's still quick to do what I tell her. Running my hands along her back, down her butt, and around to the top of her thigh, I hear her breath come out on a gasp. My hand is on the inside of her thigh, inching upward until I slide my finger into her pussy. Fuck, she is so wet for me already. The fingers on my other hand trace her front from her hip up to one of her tits, and I rub two of my fingers together, pulling on her nipple.

In the mirror across from us, I watch her lean back into me. Her soft moans make it difficult to keep from driving into her right away. Increasing the pressure of my finger against her clit, I kiss along her neck. The rougher I finger her, the louder she moans, her entire body jerking against my hand.

"I want you to watch me touch you," I whisper against her ear.

Her full lips make a perfect O as she sees her reflection. Having her not only feel what I'm doing to her body but knowing she's watching me do it is tantalizing. She stands there wide-eyed, just watching my hands. I can't take it anymore. I have to be inside her.

Moving into position, I slide my aching cock into her with enough force to make her entire body lean forward. Her pussy clenches around my cock a second before she screams my name. Her scream is music to my ears, but it's nothing compared to watching her come in the mirror. As I pound into her, I feel her body still shaking around me. Her hand reaches down to move my hand away from her pussy, but I'm not done with her yet.

"Don't make me stop." I meet her eyes in the mirror. "I want to watch myself touch your pussy while I'm fucking you."

She closes her eyes, keeping her hand over mine as I watch myself finger her while I'm sliding my cock deep inside of her. Her breath comes out on a pant and her entire body tenses. With the next hard thrust, I feel her pussy tightening around my cock again as she comes. My hands move to her hips, gripping them as my entire body jerks with my release, her muscles tightening around me, milking me dry.

Nuzzling her neck, I hold on to her tightly, not letting her move for a minute. The curator will be back soon, so I know I must release her, but it doesn't mean I really want to. With a sigh, I finally let her go. She lowers her leg and turns around.

While I love her ass, it's her face that always gets me. I rub my thumb across her full lips, staring into her captivating brown eyes. My hand follows the line of her high cheekbone until I run it through her soft hair. When her hands massage the tops of my shoulders, I catch sight of her ring.

"I love seeing my ring on your finger."

"You know, not that I'm comparing rings or anything, but yours is bigger," she says with a shit-eating grin on her face.

"How am I supposed to compete with a wolf?" I look down at her tits. "Now quit messing with me before I bend you over this chair. If you're not careful, the curator will come back to find us still naked."

My threat has her scurrying to get dressed, which part of me thinks is a terrible shame. She arches her brow, waiting for me to put on my clothes. With a sigh, I quickly dress. Unlocking the door, she grabs my hand, leading me back through the house. To get a last glimpse of her ass before we get to my parents' house, I let her walk ahead of me. She's throwing her backpack in the passenger seat of her Jeep when I come up behind her.

"I'll see you at my parents' place. Call me if you need to pull over along the way."

Grabbing her around the waist, I give her a quick kiss before getting into my SUV. I wait for her to pull out behind me as we begin our trek back to the city. About a mile down the road, I glance in my rearview mirror and she's looking down at her ring while she drives. Everything's going according to plan.

THIRTY

RACHAEL

Vonni pulls up to the guardhouse, speaking to Ben briefly before the gate opens and he drives through. Before following him up the drive, I stop next to Ben and roll my window down.

"You must be a proud poppa now, since I don't see you limping."

"The baby came Monday." He leans in the window. "Thanks for asking."

"Details, man, details. Boy or girl?"

"A healthy baby boy named Nathan." His grin is so wide, his brown eyes crinkle at the corners. "He weighed seven and a half pounds when he was born."

"Congratulations. Give your wife my best."

He's still smiling as I drive through the gate and up to the house. Vonni's standing at the back of his SUV with his arms crossed when I pull in behind him.

"What took you so long?" he asks as I get out. "I was worried that something happened at the gate."

"I noticed Ben wasn't limping, so I got baby details."

"Damn, I forgot." He rubs the back of his neck. "Now I feel like an ass."

"A healthy baby boy named Nathan." I walk up to him and kiss him on the cheek. "Just congratulate him on the way out."

He takes my hand, leading me through the house. This time there's nobody on the porch, so we head to the backyard where we hear the distinct murmur of voices, and a cheer goes up once we're spotted. Vonni's brother Rafe is the first to come up to us.

"It's not too late to marry a better looking Moran."

"I suppose I'll just have to settle for the sexiest of the Morans," I reply, giving Vonni a once over.

Rafe laughs, moving aside to make room for Christian, who eyes Vonni with disdain.

"Is this the attire I can expect from now on? You look like a fucking hippie. In fact, I'm surprised you're not wearing sandals."

Vonni's still wearing a dark blue dress shirt open at the collar and rolled up to his forearm. The jeans are more casual than his standard dress pants, but he's still wearing loafers.

"I rather like the jeans. It's a pleasant change of pace."

"You would." Christian kisses my cheek. "I knew you were trouble the moment I saw you. Seems fitting that we'll be related."

"Rachael isn't the only one with a new ring," Luke says, moving to stand next to Christian.

"How the fuck did I miss that thing, Luke?" Christian asks, looking down at Vonni's hand.

Two guys, who I've never met before, coming up on either side of Christian and Luke, stare down at Vonni's hand. Their resemblance to Christian is uncanny.

"Rachael, these are my brothers, Johnny and DJ," Christian says with a jerk of his thumb in their direction.

With a nod, I shake both of their hands.

"A wolf ring, huh?" The brother Christian introduced as Johnny razzes Vonni.

His light brown eyes sparkle with mirth, and his lips are ridiculously full for a man. Noticeably so, even around his trimmed beard.

All the guys pick on Vonni, except DJ. He has an air of brooding sensuality about him. A scar that runs from his eye to his ear does nothing to detract from his beauty. If anything, I think he's better looking than Christian. I'm sure Christian attracts more attention because of his easygoing and playful nature, while DJ seems to prefer blending into the background.

"You guys are just jealous that you were never good enough in bed for a woman to buy you a ring," Vonni says in all seriousness.

All the guys break out in laughter, joking with each other back and forth. Vonni's father, John, steps into the fold, and all the boys move back to make room for him.

"What's all the commotion about?"

Christian smirks as he points to Vonni's hand. "Rachael got him a ring too."

"Listen, I didn't know Vonni was going to propose when I bought it." I glare at the lot of them. "The wolf is lucky among my people."

John inspects the ring as he asks, "The boys have been teasing you about it, have they?"

"A bit," Vonni says, shrugging his shoulders.

"What do these wise guys know anyway?" John smiles. "It's not like women are buying them shit."

John reaches for my hand. "Let me see your ring." He gazes at it for a moment before looking into my eyes. "I always thought Vonni would take his duty to this family too seriously and never get married. I've never been happier to be wrong."

I pull John to the side and lower my voice. "I know you won't believe me, but my grandmother can sometimes see things before they happen. Her vision prompted me to take his ring to the shaman to be blessed, and while I was there, I had a similar vision. The shaman doesn't have my grandmother's abilities, but he senses things. He told me not to hesitate when the time came, or all would be lost. I think it's all connected, and Vonni's in danger."

His gaze bores into me. "What makes you think I wouldn't believe you?"

"I'm used to people thinking my grandmother is crazy, and the traditions of my people . . . odd."

He looks over the top of my head, making a forward motion with his hand. Nonno appears beside me, bending his head to kiss the hand with my engagement ring.

"I believe you, Rachael." He turns to Nonno. "Rachael brought me some information involving a threat to Vonni. She bought him the wolf ring for protection."

"Does Vonni know?"

I shake my head no and watch as the frown lines on Nonno's forehead deepen as I relay my concerns.

He turns to John. "You'll have to talk to Vonni. He's become too lax about weapons around Rachael, and her apartment. We need to double security, making sure everyone stays in groups of twos and threes."

Once John nods his agreement, he looks back at me. "Rachael, none of us can keep you safe in your apartment. Too many people coming and going. Anyone could pull off a hit. Vonni's townhouse is still not enough protection for either of you. No one is staying at my place right now. Would you be willing to move there with Vonni temporarily?"

"On one condition. I know your place is for the Morans, but I have a friend that I'd like to invite over."

"Vonni told me about your friend Chantal." Nonno's eyes crinkle at the corners. "He's no threat to any of us, so I see no reason he can't visit."

Vonni walks up to us. "What are you three so deep in conversation about?"

"I'm worried about Rachael's safety at her apartment," Nonno smoothly replies. "She has agreed to live with you, temporarily, at my old place."

Vonni gives Nonno a weird look but doesn't argue.

"Ma's complaining everyone's seen Rachael's ring but her."

Vonni takes me by the hand, leading me toward where his mom's holding court, and I hold out my hand for her inspection. She looks from me to Vonni and smiles.

"It's beautiful. We're so happy for you two."

We make the rounds, holding my hand out for all the ladies to see. Mandy's my last stop and Sebastian sits next to her with his arm across the back of her chair. Before either can comment, Elena stands up and taps her wineglass.

"Everyone come and sit. We need to pick a date for the engagement ball."

"Engagement ball?" I lean in to ask Vonni.

"It's tradition for all the families to come and give their blessing. They usually bring the couple a gift."

Everyone files around the table.

"How about two Saturdays from now?"

Soft voices confer as phones are whipped out. Nobody has anything they can't reschedule, so the date is set. Voices fire off around the table concerning who's going to call who about the details. Elena asks Johnny and DJ to hand deliver invitations once she has them ready.

I look at Elena. "What can I do to help?"

"Honey, you show up, look good, and mingle," Vonni's Aunt Carol says with the shake of her dark bob.

"I can do that."

"Rachael," Vonni's Aunt Ashley says, tucking a strand of her blond hair behind her ear. "I'd like to design your outfit for the engagement ball."

"I'd love that. I know I'm in expert hands with you dressing me and Chantal doing my hair and makeup. Lord knows, he'll tell you I need all the help I can get."

"I'd love to meet him. Bring him with you to the shop when we do a fitting."

"He'll be in heaven. You've been forewarned that he may never want to leave your shop."

Food and drinks circulate, cutting our conversation short for the moment. A glass of red wine is set before me, along with a Caesar salad. I sip the wine while waiting for everyone to get their salads. While we eat our salads, plates of lasagna are brought out. Small groups of family are laughing and talking. The obvious love and camaraderie they share fills my heart.

Vonni leans in, whispering against my ear, "What's the gigantic sigh for?"

"Just content," I say, turning to stroke my hand along his cheek.

"Let's go pack some clothes and head over to Nonno's place."

"Why don't you let me drive?" I trace the deep purple under his eyes. "Have one of the guys pick you up at Nonno's in the morning."

"That sounds good. Let's go, cara. I'm beat."

We make the rounds, saying goodbye before we head out. As we get in my Jeep, he leans back against the passenger seat and closes his eyes.

"I need you to stop by my place on the way so I can grab some things."

"Input the address in the GPS for me," I tell him as I start down the long driveway.

On the drive into the city, I listen to the sound of the British voice on the GPS and chuckle to myself. Vonni's head lolls back, soft snoring sounds coming from him within minutes. When I pull up to a brick townhouse, he comes awake with a start, looking around as if he forgot where he was for a moment.

He runs a hand over his face. "Christ, I can't believe I fell asleep."

My curiosity gets the better of me to see where he lives, although since we've been together, live might be too strong of a word. He pretty much showers and changes his clothes here.

Just inside the front door, there's a small vestibule and staircase. Vonni takes the steps two at a time up to what I assume is his bedroom. On my own, I give myself a tour of the first floor. When you stand in his living room, you can see all the way through to the kitchen at the back of the house. Everything is modern, clean, and minimal. The very back wall is nothing but windows with a door that leads out into a fenced-in backyard.

The top of the stairs opens into a large common area with two rooms to the left and one to the right. Straight ahead is an open living area, where I can tell Vonni spends most of his time. The furniture is worn leather and there's a large TV. Books are scattered across the coffee table, along with several remotes and a gaming controller.

Peeking into the first room on the left, the bed is made, and everything is pristine. The second room I come to is a bathroom done in shades of navy and gray. Everything is very masculine in the master bedroom, down to the plain navy comforter. Across from the bed is another large TV. On one nightstand sits a remote and on the other is a gaming controller. When I investigate his closet, I discover he has more clothes than any man I have ever met. All neatly hung and sorted by color.

Vonni stands at the bathroom counter, packing a travel bag with his necessities. I move past him to salivate over his large stand-alone tub with jets.

"You like the tub?"

"I'm jealous. I'd never get out."

"Nonno's place has one too. I think I'm going to enjoy walking in to find you covered in bubbles."

"As long as you promise to join me."

He raises an eyebrow but says nothing. He goes into the bedroom, throwing more things in his suitcase as I sit on his bed and watch. Opening another suitcase that's designed to hold suits, he fits several pairs of pants with matching jackets and shirts in it.

"Come on, cara, let's head to your place to pack."

Following him out, I reach down to lock the door behind us as he throws everything in the back of my Jeep.

When we reach the landing of my apartment, Chantal peeks around his door and when he sees us, he makes a beeline to my door as I'm unlocking it.

"Come chat while I pack a bag."

Vonni flops down on the sofa, laying his head back as Chantal and I go into my bedroom.

Chantal whispers, "Is he ok?"

With a nod, I dig out my dress bag and a small suitcase. "He didn't sleep much last night, then he drove all the way to my grandmother's."

"You just got back, Miss Thang." He smiles. "Where are you packing to go now?"

He squeals as I hold out my hand. "Damn, that boy got taste. That's the largest emerald I've ever seen, Ray."

"Do me a favor and tease him about his ring being bigger."

Chantal gives me a conspiratorial wink. "Naturally. Boyfriend got a ring too?"

I give him the details of my trip ending with, "Nonno says security will be easier at his place. He asked if I would stay there with Vonni for now. Just because I won't be down the hall doesn't mean you can forget about me. I want you to come see us at Nonno's."

"Girl, they can't keep me away." He envelops me in a bear hug. "BFFs for life. You aren't getting rid of me that easy."

I zip up my bags and dash into the bathroom to grab the last of what I need. Dumping my bathroom items, along with the contents of my backpack into my purse, Chantal and I head out to the living room.

At the sound of our approach, Vonni stands up and smiles. "Did she show you her ring?"

"I understand boyfriend got a ring too, let me see." Vonni

holds out his hand for Chantal's inspection. "How come yours is bigger?"

Chantal and I burst out laughing at Vonni's sputter. He realizes he's being teased and crosses his arms over his chest.

"It's not fair for the two of you to gang up on me."

"Honey, you would love it if we ganged up on you."

Before Vonni can respond, Chantal sashays out the door. Vonni shakes his head and grabs my bags so I can lock up. On the drive over to Nonno's, Vonni relaxes against the seat and when we get there, I back up to the door to make it easier to unload. Sebastian's large frame fills my rearview mirror as I come to a stop.

"What are you doing here?"

"George wasn't feeling well today, so I volunteered to come by and help you guys in case you had a lot of bags," he says with a smirk in Vonni's direction.

"Sebastian, it's temporary. How much stuff do you think we have?"

"I've taken trips with Vonni before." He grabs my bags out of the back. "I think he packed light so you wouldn't think he's a freak."

Vonni gives Sebastian a dark look before leading the way upstairs. Running my hand over the exposed brick, I walk around, looking out the window. From up here, the view is pretty. A long sloping lawn ends at a thick line of trees.

When I turn from the window, I notice the giant four-poster bed in dark wood. The comforter is a floral print in shades of blue and green on a red background. When I open the large armoire across from it, I find a TV and gaming system, with the lower drawers designed for clothing. A second large armoire stands between two doors. One door leads to a small closet, and the other door to an enormous bathroom with a walk-in shower and Jacuzzi tub.

"Vonni, I'm going to enjoy staying at Nonno's."

"Told you," he says as he leans against the doorjamb. "Don't tell anyone, but Nonno keeps bubble bath under the sink. Might tarnish his reputation."

"Really? At his age? I thought he's retired."

Vonni stands there looking deep in thought, as if he's trying to decide what to say.

"Nonno stepped down to let Pop run things, but he started the family. To this day, his rules are still followed. Just because Nonno looks like a cute old man, doesn't mean he isn't the most lethal of all of us. He grew up in the streets, building this family from nothing. He understands things in a way that Pop and I never will."

When I follow him into the bedroom, I see he's already unpacked our suitcases and throw them to the side to make room on the bed for him to lie down. I watch as he unbuttons his shirt, tossing it on the back of a chair. He withdraws a handgun from the back of his pants, setting it on the bedside table, before he takes them off and crawls into bed. It's a little unnerving to know how comfortable he is handling a gun.

Nonno's right. He's been lax about weapons since this is the first time I've ever seen him with a gun. With a sinking feeling, I know he's been trying to shelter me from the unpleasant aspects of who he is. That ideal has been shattered.

THIRTY-ONE

VONNI

Ties, I fucking hate them. The only thing that can get me in one is a wedding, funeral, or, in this case, a meeting of the commission. Pop and I are sitting in my SUV parked across the street from a bakery in the heart of Little Italy. At least Cake My Day looks like your run-of-the-mill bakery. The name is quite genius considering it's owned by Lucia Russo, wife of mob boss Frankie Russo. Frankie and Nonno came up in the business together. For the last thirty-some years, the commission meetings have always been held in a secret room at the back of the bakery.

Antonio Corleone, the boss of the Vineta family, opens the glass door to go in. There are only two bosses left not yet in attendance, Pop and Vito.

Looking down at my watch, I ask Pop, "How long are you going to wait to see if he shows?"

"These meetings aren't optional, Vonni. He'll be here."

"You're right, Pop. Vito's getting out of his car now." I nod my head toward the royal blue town car pulling up in front of the bakery. "How do you want to play this?"

"You'll see once we get inside." After Vito goes inside, Pop reaches for his car door. "Remember, you're here to observe only. You don't have a spot on the commission yet. Don't speak unless spoken to."

With a curt nod, I get out. Following behind Pop, my eyes scan the street for anything out of place. The tinkle of a chime sounds as we go through the front door. Pop gives the teenage girl behind the tall glass counter a nod before going through a swinging door marked employees only.

There isn't a soul in the humongous modern kitchen. Pop keeps going until he reaches another door labeled storage and goes in. The label isn't misleading, we're in a tiny storeroom that holds shelves of baking goods and equipment.

"Shut the door behind us."

Once the door swings shut, Pop meets my eyes before grabbing a black handheld blender on the middle shelf. The entire back wall swings out to reveal a lit cement tunnel.

From inside, Pop presses a button on the wall and the panel swings shut behind us. The tunnel's narrow and when I try to stand up, I hit my head on the ceiling. We don't have to hunch over for long though, because it opens up into a rectangular boardroom. All the men sitting at the polished wood conference table look up at us. Pop goes around the table, shaking hands, and speaking to each individual while I hang back, leaning against the wall.

Standing there, I let my eyes wander around the room. A fully stocked bar stands at one end, and a big screen TV hangs on the wall at the opposite end. This room could have been any fortune five hundred company boardroom. All that's missing is a frazzled assistant passing out food. A gavel banging on the table catches my attention.

Frankie stands at the head of the table, gavel in hand. Before he can say anything, Vito speaks up from across the table.

"What is Vonni doing here? He's not a boss."

"He's underboss, and my successor." Pop meets the eyes of all five men before inclining his head at Marco. "Vonni is here in the capacity of observer only. I didn't want his first introduction to the commission to be under the same set of circumstances as Marco's. He knows all the men in this room and is involved in every aspect of the family business."

All the men in the room bow their heads in agreement, except for Vito. Meeting Vito's eyes, I keep my face blank. Internally, I'm smiling at the fucker. It gives me great satisfaction that he's the first to look away.

"Let's get on with it, then." Frank gives Pop a nod. "I'm opening up the floor."

"Has anyone else had increased surveillance?" Antonio asks from his spot next to Vito.

No one says anything for a minute, sitting there, watching each other.

"Agents Fitzsimmons and Keller have taken an unusual interest in Charlotte." Marco clears his throat. "It's nothing I've been concerned about because she won't be able to tell them anything they don't already know."

"Vonni." Domenico Fossera, of the Ricci family, meets my eyes. When I tilt my head, he continues, "Have they been following Rachael as well?"

"Not that we've seen yet." I push off the wall and step forward to make sure all the men can hear me. "They have a passing curiosity only. I expect that will change since it's only a matter of time before they hear about our engagement. Rachael has already thought about the possibility of being questioned by police. She and I have an agreement that things are on a need-to-know basis, and she will not be involved in the family business. Like Charlotte, she knows nothing of value."

When I look around the table, all the men seem to accept my answer and have no further questions. Just as I'm about to take my place against the wall again, Antonio speaks up.

"How about you, Vonni? Are they following you any more

than they ever have?"

"According to Sebastian's guy inside the FBI, Fields has been appointed to put together a task force to end organized crime. Fields is more interested in getting a promotion than a financial windfall. His game plan is to take out upper-level individuals, in the hopes the whole thing collapses with us in jail. I think it's safe to assume we should all plan to be watched more closely."

All the men wear matching expressions of concern except Pop, who heard about it from Sebastian a few days ago. No one else speaks up, so I go back to my post against the wall.

"John, do we have a way to get to Fields?" Frank asks.

"Not easily." Pop lets out a sigh. "It will be next to impossible to turn him. We go after either him or his family directly, and I'm afraid it'll only bring more heat. I'm recommending for now at least, we do nothing."

"Nothing, that's your solution!"

Vito stands, his palms smacking against the table. Pop doesn't flinch. He sits there eyeing Vito, as if he's bored.

"Playing along gives you time to find your enemy's weakness and have a well thought out plan of attack." He looks around the table, pausing. "Which brings me to my next order of business. I move we end our relationship with Fred from the local 79 and kick everything to Will from zoning."

Frank sits forward. "Why?"

"Would you like to field that one, Vito?"

Pop's face is blank. He's thrown down the gauntlet in front of the entire commission. A bead of sweat gathering on Vito's brow is the only tell of the dangerous situation he finds himself in. You could hear a pin drop while everyone stares at Vito, waiting to see what he'll say.

"On my suggestion, Fred gave Vonni an incorrect bid." Everyone shifts in their chairs. "Thankfully, Vonni was quick to figure that out. When it was brought to my attention, unfortunately, I knew my suspicions about Fred were correct. I not only second the move from Fred to Will, but I also move we take further action."

Fucker can think on his feet, I'll give him that.

THIRTY-TWO

RACHAEL

When I poke my head into Kendra's office to say goodbye, she gives me a distracted wave while staring at her computer screen. In the elevator on the way down, I remember I have to tell Chantal about Ashley's offer to design my outfit for the engagement ball. On the way to my Jeep, I have my head down, texting Chantal when I bump into someone. I mumble "sorry" without even looking up and open my door.

"Rachael LaDeuc?" a deep voice asks.

That catches my attention. The biker guy I saw at the diner on the day I met Vonni stares down at me. Eyeing him, I decide he's better suited to biker attire than the navy blazer and khaki pants he has on today. Vonni told me he was a veteran of the FBI. This can't be good.

"Yes. What can I do for you?"

"I'm agent Kyle Fitzsimmons with the FBI." His blue eyes are like twin shards of cut glass. His name seems more fitting for an investment banker than an FBI agent. "You'll have to put your dinner plans on hold and come with me."

"And if I don't?"

I let my statement hang in the air between us.

"Look, I can come back tomorrow and formally question you at work. However, I don't think you want me to do that. It's better for both of us if we keep things quiet."

"Today it is, then." I make a sweeping gesture with my hand. "Lead the way."

He opens the back door of his navy Crown Victoria, which I can't help but notice is parked right next to my Jeep. He shuts the door behind me with a soft click, walking around to the driver's side.

"You'll have to forgive me, but I'm a first timer. How does this work?" I ask after he gets in.

"Well, I bring you to HQ and you agree to become an informant." He watches me in his rearview mirror. "In exchange, we offer you protection and little to no jail time."

"What if I plead the fifth?"

"We build a case against you, alongside the rest of the Morans."

"That's a little hard to do when I have broken no laws."

He shrugs as if he doesn't believe for a second that's true. "We'll see."

We pull up to a nondescript tan three story building with no visible signage on the outside. The lobby is huge and there's a security desk complete with metal detectors, but no one is there monitoring them.

Agent Fitzsimmons steers me to a bank of elevators on the right. The ding when we arrive at the third floor grates on my already frayed nerves. When we get off the elevator, we pass cubicle after cubicle. The few agents that are still hard at work stare at me as if I have a horn growing out of my head. Finally, I'm shown into an empty office at the end of the hallway with a nameplate on the desk that says Jeff Fields, Director.

"Sit here and wait," Agent Fitzsimmons says, leaving me by myself.

Not sure if this is some kind of tactic or test, I sit there looking around. Two large Ficus plants sit on either side of the dark brown credenza. Animal skulls line the top of it, and a row of cacti sits on the windowsill. The most disturbing of all is the human skull that sits on the corner of his desk.

After thirty minutes, the thought of hailing a cab crosses my mind when a tall man in a navy suit sails into the office and sits down. He's thin with short sandy blond hair and piercing blue eyes. His seventies style mustache does not match the look he wants to portray with that suit. He watches me in silence for a moment, sitting with his hands steepled together. I'm pretty sure it's an intimidation method, and it's working. My phone ringing breaks the silence.

"If it's Vonni, assure him you're fine and you have to work late," he says in a calm monotone voice.

With a nod, I pick up the phone.

"Hey babe, I'll be home soon." I look around Field's office, trying to figure out a clue I can give him about my whereabouts when inspiration strikes. "I got caught up in reviewing federal contracts for Kendra."

"Fields has you, doesn't he?"

Vonni catches onto my hint right away, knowing that nothing I do for Kendra involves federal contracts.

"Yeah, you know, standard stuff." I try to keep an even tone despite my case of nerves, so he won't worry. "Tell George to hold dinner for me."

"Answer whatever questions they ask." The sound of his sigh makes me picture him pinching the bridge of his nose. "You know nothing, and you broke no laws."

With a dial tone in my ear, I hang up the phone and meet Field's gaze.

"Well, I'm not on a timetable. Ask me whatever you want to."

"Tell me about your relationship with Vonni."

"It's quicker if you tell me what you know, and I'll fill in the blanks."

I swallow around the lump in my throat, trying to project

an air of confidence I wasn't feeling.

"Fair enough." He leans back. "You met by chance in a diner and have been together ever since. Word is out that you're engaged. You have no criminal record or priors. What I don't get is, why?"

"Does anyone ever ask you why you married your wife?" I point to his wedding band. "My guess is no. You married her because you fell in love with her."

He leans forward. "So, you're telling me you fell in love with a gangster?"

"Crazier things have happened."

I lean forward as well, matching his posture.

He taps his chin with his finger. "Do you even know how his family makes money?"

"I only had two conditions for Vonni." I hold up my fingers, ticking off items as I speak. "The first was fidelity, and the second was not to be involved in the family's business. He's upheld his end of the bargain. If you're hoping I can provide you information through pillow talk, I'm afraid you're out of luck. I know nothing of interest, even if I am inclined to help you."

"You've been to John Morans house?" His fingers are once again steepled. "Met the family?"

"I think you already know the answer to that question."

I lean back, crossing my arms over my chest.

"Will you be going back again soon?"

He watches me like he expects to catch me in a lie, and I know he'll never believe that I don't even have anything to lie about. At first, I consider not bringing up the engagement ball, but then I realize that's useless. Even if their surveillance is only subpar, he probably knows about the ball, anyway.

"Next weekend for our engagement ball."

"Perfect. All the players will be there. Agent Fitzsimmons will set you up with a wire."

THIRTY-THREE

VONNI

"Pop, we have a situation."

I lean against the tree outside, running the tips of my fingers over my grandparents' initials.

"What's going on?"

The sound of his gruff voice helps calm the anger churning in my gut.

"Fitzsimmons grabbed Rachael when she left work today and took her downtown. Fields interviewed her about our relationship and the family." Rachael speaking to the FBI isn't cause for concern, since she knows nothing that can hurt us. The next part, however, is another matter. "He wants her to wear a wire to the engagement ball."

"Is she all right?"

"Yeah, but I could kill that fucker for humiliating her. It galls me she felt she had to justify our relationship to that prick."

"Hmm. The wire is a complication. One that we can manage with a few discreet phone calls. Right now, they don't have shit on her, but if she refuses to wear the wire, they can haul her in for impeding an investigation. I'd rather not start a pissing contest with the FBI if we can avoid it."

"I'll let Rachael know."

Hanging up the phone, I push off the tree and head inside. Rachael isn't by the bar, so I head to her next favorite spot, Nonno's old office. Instead of finding her dark head bent over a book, the room is empty. I jog upstairs and once I'm in our room, I hear running water. Turning on my heel, I head back downstairs to the bar, pouring a glass of wine for her and a double shot of cognac for myself.

When I walk into the bathroom, Rachael's resting against the back of the tub with her eyes closed. A thick layer of bubbles along the surface hides her luscious body from my view. I stand there watching her, anyway. She has naturally tanned, flawless skin. Chantal does her makeup sometimes, but she doesn't need him to. She looks just as irresistible without it.

"Are you going to stare at me all day, or are you going to get in?"

She still has her eyes closed, but her lip turns up at the corner. Originally, I was going to have a cocktail with her while I told her about my conversation with Pop. Now I'm thinking about putting her smart mouth to good use first.

Carefully, I set the drinks on the edge of the tub. The sound of my zipper has her eyes snapping open. Standing before her in my boxer briefs and dress shirt, I slowly undo the top couple of buttons. Her eyes are glued to my hands until I lift my shirt over my head. She lingers on my chest before lowering her gaze to my abs. When her eyes land on my cock, it strains toward her through my boxers. Her eyes flash to my hands again when I reach for the waistband. Once I release my cock, she stares at it, moistening her lips with her pink tongue.

"See anything you want?"

I move forward until my cock is damn near touching her

lips. Her tongue juts out to lick the head and I can't help the low moan that escapes me. She sits up straighter in the tub. The bubbles slide down to reveal her perfect tits just as she swallows the head of my cock. Her mouth slides all the way to the base of my dick, and I feel my head rub against the back of her throat. I slide my hands into her short dark hair and fuck her mouth. Water sloshes over my feet, but I could give a fuck. She's sexy as hell, her tits bouncing as she takes me into her mouth.

Pulling out of her mouth, I look into her eyes. "Sit on the edge of the tub and spread your legs wide. I want to taste you."

She's quick to do as I ask, getting out of the tub. I go to my knees before her, getting ready to worship the sweetest tasting pussy I've ever had. Her nails dig into my scalp as I suck hard on her clit just the way she likes. Her moans make me crazy, but it's not enough. When I slide my finger into her wet pussy and begin fucking her with it, she screams, pulling my hair.

I sit back in the tub, pulling her on top of me and with a hand on each ass cheek I thrust into her. Her head is thrown back and her lids are heavy as she rides me. Her tits bounce up and down in front of my face as she takes my cock. Removing one of my hands from her ass, I grab the underside of her tit, positioning her nipple perfectly. I suck hard, feeling her body tense around me. Fuck, nothing feels better than when my girl comes all over me and as the last of her tremors subside, mine begin. Holding her tightly, I come deep inside of her.

When I open my eyes, she's looking around the bathroom, a smile on her full lips. "We made a big water mess, Vonni."

"Cara, to be quite honest, I could not care less right now."

My heart is still beating wildly, and my dick hasn't even quit twitching. A meteor could hit the house and I'd die one happy fucker. I push back with my feet until I can lean back against the side of the tub. I'm happy to see the drinks are still where I left them, and I hand her the wine before I grab my cognac.

As I sip on my drink, I watch her. She's still astride my cock, and her tits are eye level. Exactly where I want her.

Her head tilts to the side as she watches me. "What did John say?"

"He thinks the inconvenience of the wire is manageable."

She worries her bottom lip with her teeth. I know she's getting worked up over a potentially dangerous situation that she has no control over. Damn if she doesn't look sexy doing it. Her eyes go wide as my dick swells inside of her and taking her glass from her, I set it aside. Time to distract her.

THIRTY-FOUR

RACHAEL

I run my hand down a row of Nonno's old books, trying to figure out what I'm going to read while I wait for Chantal. The scent of Vonni's cigar from last night still lingers in the air. The entire office has always smelled masculine, and maybe that's why it's my favorite room. Leather, wood, brick, and the faint scent of alcohol all mingle together. My favorite scent in here is Vonni's musk. It's like a mix of forest, cinnamon, and something wholly him.

Finally, he's made himself comfortable in Nonno's old office, and it suits him. At first, he wouldn't use this room because he knows how much I like it in here, but he needed an office, and I can read in any room. A random trip with Mandy to an antique store gave him the push he needed.

We came home with a desk lamp, beverage cart, and cigar box complete with ashtray. The brass lamp gives off a nice soft glow, more for looks than anything else. It reminds me of something you'd see in a western or a 1950s sitcom. Heck, the thing might even be from that time. The beverage cart is all brass, complete with matching ice bucket and tongs that thrill me for some strange reason. George understood my fascination and was quick to help me clean it up and stock it. The cigar box is Vonni's favorite, I think. It's rather heavy and made from cedar. It folds out to hold cigars, a lighter, and a cigar cutter. In the store, I never opened it, but Vonni found a brass lighter and cigar cutter inside.

Standing behind the desk, I look through the titles on the bookshelf. Curiously, there's one hardcover in the middle of the paperbacks. When I pull it off the shelf, the spine feels old and fragile. When I open it, I see a man's bold scribble sprawled across a blank white page. It's addressed to Raine, Vonni's grandmother. It might be a private note, and I freeze, but curiosity trumps my moral quandary.

I'm shit with telling you how I feel, so I got all the great poets to do it for me.

Giovanni

When I thumb through the book, there are love poems from some of the greats—Elizabeth Barrett Browning, Robert Burns, and William Shakespeare. From out in the hall, I hear voices and I smile as I put the book back in the same place. If bubble bath isn't good for Nonno's reputation, I doubt a book of love poems he gave to his wife is going to help. Nonchalantly, I lean my hip against the desk, waiting for Vonni and whoever he was with to walk in.

"Cara, I wasn't expecting you to still be home." Vonni raises his eyebrow. "Aren't you going dress shopping with Chantal?"

Thankfully, my phone buzzes from the desk.

"The office is all yours." On my way out, I kiss his cheek. "He just texted me, he's out front." I smile as I pass Rafe. "Good to see you again."

Quickly, I shut the door behind me before Vonni can ask me questions. I'm pretty sure I look guilty, and I'm a terrible liar.

"Aren't you a sight for sore eyes, Miss Thang," Chantal says, leaning over the center console to hug me.

"I'm so glad to see you." I squeeze him so hard I feel his breath come out in a whoosh. "It feels like it's been years."

"You look beautiful, as always." We both know that's not true today. I'm wearing worn jeans and a T-shirt with Lionel Richie's face on it. He eyes me as he's pulls out of the driveway. "I know something's off, you might as well tell me."

"I'm not sure which thing you're speaking of. The fact that I just found hidden love poems from Nonno or the FBI making me wear a wire to the engagement party."

His dark eyes bulge out. "Does Vonni know?"

"About the love poems, no. That secret stays between you, me, and Nonno. About the FBI, of course. I would never betray Vonni. I don't know anything, and I haven't broken any laws. For my safety, John thinks it best we play along."

He watches me out of the corner of his eye as he drives. "What does that mean?"

"It means everyone in the place will be warned ahead of time that I'm wearing a wire. I'm pretty sure they are smart enough not to say anything around an unfamiliar girl, anyway. It's a celebration, not a business meeting."

"Am I allowed to say I'm relieved? You give them something. Not the something they're hoping for, but enough to get you off the hook."

"I doubt I'll be off the hook, but John thinks it will pacify them for now."

Looking out the window, I hope John is right.

"I knew it."

"You knew what?"

"That Nonno's a closet romantic."

Both of us are giggling as we pull up in front of Ashley's store in the heart of the garment district. At this hour, her shop is the only one with lights still on. I'm pretty sure Chantal sees her lights as a homing beacon, since he's pulling hard on my arm. Mannequins line the inside of the window, and one outfit catches my eye. Chantal looks from me to the window.

"Oh my god, Ray." He bounces up and down. "Do you think she can make us matching outfits? I'm just saying, we'd both look fierce in that red romper."

"It's gorgeous," I say, almost pressing my face against the glass. The top of the romper is strapless with a plunging v neck. Even though it's one piece, the top looks like a large ruffle that flows around the waist of the pants. "You would look fierce, I'd probably look like a red Oompa Loompa."

"Girl, you so crazy." He laughs. "Come on, I'm dying to see what she designed for you."

Chantal is like a kid in a candy store, and there's no holding him back. He's running wild, touching every swatch of fabric in the store that he comes to.

"You can only touch one more, then we have to find Ashley."

"Too late, you found her."

"Crap." I sigh. "I warned you, he's never going to want to leave. Your store is like his Mecca."

In the time it takes for Ashley to sneak up on me, I no longer even see Chantal. Oh, but I can hear him.

"Damn, let me look through these boxes and see if this comes in a ten."

With a half-hearted groan, I cover my face with my hands.

"He'll be fine, let him look around while you try on your dress. I'm an excellent seamstress, so I have plenty of time to let it out or take it in."

Ashley takes my hand and pulls me past the bolts of fabric and a row of mannequins, stopping at the dressing rooms and pointing to the first one.

"I hung it up in there already."

When I step in and close the door, I come face to face with an elegant emerald green gown. I run my hand over the sleek material, admiring the cut of the fabric. It's designed to hang off my shoulders with the neckline plunging into my cleavage. It has an empire waist that transitions into a flowing floor-length skirt.

When I walk out of the dressing room, Ashley's standing there. She looks at me critically, moving around me, adjusting my limbs as she inspects the dress.

"I can't believe it, I don't have to tailor a thing."

"No honey, you don't," Chantal says, coming to stand in front of me. He turns to Ashley. "Girl, I love your place."

"It's good to put a face with a name," Ashley says, extending her hand for him to shake.

He envelops her in a tight hug as he says, "Honey, we family now."

Releasing her, he walks around me, not being nearly as particular or thorough as Ashley. While he's looking me over, Ashley slides a heavy gold bracelet on my wrist. The detailing is intricate, parts of the gold going from very dull to extremely shiny. Next, she hands me tear drop earrings to put in my ears. They are a heavily embroidered dull gold on the outside with emeralds on the inside.

I stand in front of the trifold mirror and slip into gold metallic platform pumps that are so shiny I swear when I look down, I'll be able to see my reflection.

Chantal lets out a sigh that catches in his throat from behind me. When I meet his gaze in the mirror, I see him wiping underneath his heavy lashes.

THIRTY-FIVE

VONNI

The windows of my SUV are dark, so the FBI won't see me giving them the finger as I drive past their van. It's juvenile, but it makes me feel better. Can they be any less obvious? A floral van, in an upscale residential area, at six thirty at night. I certainly hope they do a better job of concealing Rachael's wire than they do trying to be inconspicuous.

Ben pops out of the guard shack as soon as I pull up to my parents' gate. "Well, aren't you looking spiffy. Bow tie and everything."

"It came with the tux." I smirk and wave my hand in his direction. "They got you in a monkey suit tonight too."

"Yeah, I'm not crazy about it." He winks. "The wife likes it, though." He leans in the door and keeps his voice low. "Fields is an asshat to mess with a nice girl like Rachael. The guard shack is fully stocked should there be any trouble tonight."

"Thanks for saying so." I run my hand through my hair and sigh. "Let's hope everything goes smoothly tonight. That's all we need is the FBI breathing down our necks."

With a curt nod, he goes back to his post, and the gate swings open. There's already a valet ready to take my keys when I pull up in front.

Sebastian's booming voice is the first thing I hear when I walk in.

"Mandy, not that you don't look fucking hot, but that gown is a little revealing, isn't it?"

Leaning against the wall, I watch my sister run her hands over Sebastian's shoulders, trying to calm him down.

"You think I look hot," she purrs. She pokes her lip out, looking innocently up at him. "I saw it in a magazine and had to have it."

Damn, she's good. I didn't want to have to break it to Sebastian, she's already been running roughshod over Pop all these years. He doesn't stand a chance in hell. I breeze past them, not bothering to slow down when I hear Sebastian call out from behind me.

"Vonni, tell your sister to change before everyone gets here."

"Have fun with your argument," I call out over my shoulder and keep walking.

No way am I getting in the middle of that shit, even if Sebastian has a point. The front of the dress is a deep V that ends right above her belly button.

Rounding the corner toward Pop's office, I can hear him talking, but I'm not close enough to understand what he's saying. When I walk through the door, he's sitting behind his desk and Nonno's in front of him with his leg crossed over his knee. I pull out the other cream-colored cushy chair next to Nonno and sink into it.

"Your father was just filling me in on the commission meeting."

Nonno turns his head toward me, his eyes darkening.

"Vito's been a problem for a long time. Unfortunately, we don't have shit on him we can take to the commission to get permission to have him taken out. We know he didn't have suspicions about shit. He thought he could take the bid without us finding out, so he did."

"He's greedy and reckless, which is bad for business." Pop opens a drawer in his desk, pulling out three glasses and a fifth of whiskey. "We just have to be patient." He slides Nonno and I, our glasses. "He will fuck up, eventually. I just hope it's before any permanent damage is done."

"Agreed." Swirling around the liquid in his glass, Nonno asks Pop, "What about the FBI?"

"I'm afraid that's also a wait and see game." Pop sighs. "I hate having all this shit up in the air that we can't do anything about."

"I'm glad you're boss, not me." Nonno has a far off look in his eyes. "Law enforcement was less organized back in my day. They had a code too. Wives and children were off limits."

He shakes his head as if to clear it and turns to me. "Don't you worry about Rachael, Vonni. She's tenacious. She'll do just fine in our world."

"She better, Nonno, because I'll never let her go."

Pop and Nonno give each other a look before smiling at one another. The men in our family may be less than law-abiding citizens, but no one can ever say we don't fiercely love and protect what's ours.

"Seems to me she shares the sentiment." Nonno meets my eyes. "She went to a lot of trouble to protect you. Both her and her grandmother."

"Nonno, what are you talking about? What does her grandmother have to do with anything? I only met her once, and she told me I was late."

"Rachael still hasn't told you everything, has she?" Nonno impatiently waves his hand in my direction. "Boy, get your head out of your ass. Her grandmother sees things before they happen. Why do you think Rachael went to the trouble of having that ring blessed? It's a good thing I'm no fool. DJ has been following you since the day she told me you were in danger."

THIRTY-SIX

RACHAEL

Vonni got ready early and went ahead of me, making sure the FBI sees him arrive at his parents' house. Chantal did my hair and makeup before going home to get ready himself. Vonni thought it would be helpful for me to have a familiar face in the crowd. He not only has Nonno's blessing, but all the Morans. Chantal's become a well-liked regular within the family. Christian even volunteered to pick him up.

There's a brisk rap at the bedroom door.

"Come in."

With one last look at my reflection in the bathroom mirror, I walk into the bedroom.

"Vonni said you were driving yourself." George peeks in. "I thought if you're ready we can leave the house together."

George has been with Nonno for a long time. Not being one to break tradition, I made it a condition that he can stay with us for as long as he wants. Truth be told, I find him both endearing and comforting.

"I have to make a stop on the way, so pull out first."

He takes my arm, helping me down the stairs and out to my car. Gravel really is a pain in heels, I will have to remember to ask Vonni to pave it. Settling me in the Jeep, he heads off toward his car.

I try to hold myself together. It won't be good if I give myself away by sweating through my beautiful silk dress. My knuckles are white from gripping the wheel so hard as I pull in behind a floral van at the designated meeting point. Kyle opens the back doors of the van and holds out a hand to help me in. The girl in the khaki pants from the diner sits in back with headphones on and a laptop balanced on her knees.

Kyle nods in her direction. "You remember agent Lisa Keller?"

"Sure. If it weren't for her, I probably never would have paid any attention to Vonni and Christian at all."

"Why am I not surprised?" He blows out a breath. "Have you ever worn a wire before?"

"What do you think?"

He slides a black piece of plastic about the size and shape of a dollar piece into my cleavage. It gives me great pleasure that he's so uncomfortable doing it.

"Testing," he whispers above my cleavage.

Agent Keller gives him a thumbs up and he helps me out of the van.

Sam is standing at his usual post at the guard gate, and I give him a wide grin as I pull up. "Evening, Sam, how's the family?"

"Couldn't be better, thanks for asking."

He opens the gate, waving me through, my stomach a ball of nerves on the drive up to the house. I'm getting ready to meet every gangster in the city, along with their significant others, wearing a wire. Even with the advanced warning, anything can go wrong with the FBI listening in.

"They have you on Rachael duty?" I ask Rafe as he offers me his arm while the parking attendant comes for my car.

"I volunteered to take you and Chantal around until Vonni

gets out of his meeting with Pops. Chantal got here a minute ago, let's go find him and Christian."

Twinkle lights hang all throughout the house, and furniture has been pushed to the sides to accommodate everyone. Christian stands off to the right, bending down to hear something Chantal's saying before throwing his head back in laughter. Chantal looks regal in a dark navy tux, offering me a sweeping bow as I approach. He's lost his customary long eyelashes and makeup, which makes me sad, but I appreciate the effort he's making for the occasion.

"You look very handsome tonight. Not as stunning as you do in a red dress, but what can we do?"

"Thanks, girl." He whispers, "Vonni sent the tux over to my apartment."

Christian frowns. "What? I don't look handsome."

"So damn needy," Chantal says, eyeing him before turning back to me.

"You have no idea." Rafe grins. "Come on, we'll start on this side and work our way around."

He looks behind us, waving at a gentleman who appears to be in his sixties. His traditional black tux strains against his ample girth, a red rose sticking out of the lapel. The woman he's with is stunning in a red cocktail dress. By all appearances, she's only in her forties with long dark hair and red lipstick that's been applied perfectly to her ample lips.

Rafe shakes hands with the gentleman before bending over the lady's hand to place one chaste kiss on the back. "Antonio and Isabelle Corleone, may I introduce Vonni's fiancée, Rachael LaDeuc, and her best friend, Chantal Wade."

Shaking hands with both, I turn to Isabelle. "I love your lipstick."

Chantal leans toward her. "You'll have to tell us where you got it."

"It's Charlotte Tilbury."

Her faint Italian accent somehow makes her even more appealing. Exotic, almost.

As Rafe steers us toward the next couple, Chantal hurriedly whispers against my ear, "Charlotte Tilbury is very exclusive. I bet that lipstick set her back a hundred dollars."

"Everything that broad buys sets Ant back," Rafe whispers from my other side.

We try to smother our giggles as we get closer to an older couple that's about Nonno's age. The man is tall and thin with a full head of thick gray hair. The woman standing next to him has on a floor-length sparkly navy gown and pale blond hair that is pulled back in a tight chignon. Rafe again shakes hands with him, before placing a kiss on her hand.

"Frankie and Lucia Russo, may I introduce you to Rachael LaDeuc and Chantal Wade."

There's something warm and sweet about Lucia that I find endearing, and we speak briefly about how I met Vonni before Rafe steers us toward a couple that's only about my age.

The man's every bit as tall as Christian, but not as lean, and the woman he's with is a willowy blonde with blue eyes and fair skin. Instead of shaking hands, Rafe embraces both before turning to us.

"Marco and Charlotte Bianchi, you've heard me talk about Rachael LaDeuc. Come to think of it, I'm sure you've heard about Chantal Wade. He's become a regular around our family."

Marco brings me in for a hug before pushing me back and looking me up and down. "So, you're the girl who caught Vonni?"

"Don't pay him any mind." His wife punches him in the arm before embracing me. "He's still in shock we're at an engagement ball for Vonni. I guess we all wrote him off."

Vonni walks up, embracing Marco before turning to kiss Charlotte on the cheek. "You still haven't been able to do anything with him, huh?"

She shrugs. "Men."

"Preach it, girl," Chantal says, shaking his head emphatically.

"I went to school with Marco, and Rafe is best friends with his brother Nico," Vonni says, turning to me.

I look up at Marco with great interest. "Tell me a story about you and Vonni as kids."

"Vonni and I didn't get along as kids. I was wild, and well, Vonni has always been serious." He shakes his head. "One night I got drunk at a bar by myself. I thought because of who my dad was, I could say and do whatever the hell I wanted. A group of bikers was determined to show me otherwise. They all jumped me, and I thought I was done for until Vonni and Sebastian came out of nowhere and started throwing guys off me. Out of the one eye that wasn't swollen shut, I saw Vonni drop a guy twice his size and my mouth fell open. We've been friends ever since."

"Marco kept coming into the bar I worked at," Charlotte says. "Each time he would ask me out, even though I kept turning him down. One day Vonni came in with him and got up to sing karaoke. It was the most god-awful rendition of *Lady in Red* I'd ever heard. He threatened to keep singing it over and over until I agreed to go out with Marco."

"One day you'll have to sing for us." Chantal elbows me in the ribs. "Isn't that right, Ray?"

"Oh, yes." I look up at Vonni from under my lashes. "Humiliating yourself to get your friend a date is pretty cool."

"It was all he would fucking talk about." Vonni shrugs. "I had to do something before I lost it." He waves at someone over my head. "Come on, I'm being summoned."

Marco turns to look and see who's summoning Vonni. "You better hurry, he won't signal you a second time."

Vonni takes my hand and motions for Chantal to follow us. With his stand in duties over, Rafe hangs back with Marco.

Vonni's dad, John, is similar in age and build to the gentleman who summoned him. The dark gray of his tux matches his eyes and his dark hair is slicked back, not a hair out of place. The woman with him has straight mousy brown hair that hangs down her shoulders and with her pale complexion the silver floor-length gown she's wearing washes her out. He naturally commands attention, whereas she melts into the background behind him.

"I'm Domenico Fossera." He holds out his hand and nods his head at the plain-looking woman with him. "And this is my wife, Marie."

"I'm Rachael LaDeuc." I smile and shake both of their hands, moving aside to make room for Chantal. "This is my best friend, Chantal Wade."

"Good to see you, Dom," Vonni says, shaking his hand. "Pop was looking for you earlier. Said something about you promising him a stogie?"

"I got something from Cuba to celebrate." He grins. "I'll have to find him after dinner."

His smile slips a little and I follow his line of sight. Vito is heading toward us through the crowd.

"Dom, Marie, Vonni, and the lovely Rachael."

He takes my hand, making a show of kissing the back, which gives me the creeps.

"Chantal Wade, I'd like you to meet Vito Cordone."

John's voice projects from where he's standing in the back doorway. "If everyone will move outside, dinner is about to be served."

As we all move outside, Vonni places his hand on the small of my back. The twinkle lights continue outside, strung across the top of a large white tent that stretches the width of the backyard. Elena raises her hand, motioning to us from the back of the tent where she's surrounded by her sisters.

We pass small tables with white tablecloths and candles in the center as we make our way to her. Leaving Vonni to introduce Chantal to his aunts, Elena pulls me to the side to introduce her sisters' husbands. Pete of course I know from the docks, and we just nod at each other. John walks up with two men I haven't met before, introducing me to Carol's husband Ray and Jan's husband Carlo before telling everyone to take a seat.

Vonni comes up behind me, steering me to a table where Chantal is already talking to Sebastian and Mandy. The three of them are deep in conversation when we sit down.

His breath tickles my ear as he leans over in his seat. "You look good enough to eat, cara."

His voice sends shivers down my spine. Catching his eye, I point with my eyes down to my cleavage, silently mouthing "their listening." He laughs, trailing his hand down into my cleavage, rubbing his thumb over the device.

"The government can monitor my love life all they want. I'll be happy to give them something to talk about."

He lets the device go, throwing his arm across the back of the chair as servers come around with drink carts carrying every manner of alcohol you could want. Sebastian and Vonni purposely keep the conversation flowing, steering it toward mundane topics and Chantal of course is a source of amusement for the table. My muscles relax a little as the main course of rigatoni with vodka sauce is served.

As the servers bring cannoli out, people stop by the table and introduce themselves. Once we've had our dessert, Vonni takes my hand, leading me back inside.

"Let's stand over here to make it easier for people to approach us."

"There's a lot more people than I expected. I thought there were six families total?"

"Think of it like a pyramid structure. The top is the boss who runs his family. Below him would be an underboss or second in command, if you will. Some families have a consigliere or adviser to the boss. After them you have the capos, then the soldiers. All of them were invited, along with their significant others. Some families only came with a small contingent, but others brought everyone."

"When you said families, I assumed they were all related somehow. None of the people with Vito are related, though."

"There's only the Bianchis and us that operate that way. The Morans keep to themselves, and few outsiders are allowed. Marco took over for his father after he was killed. That was the night I didn't come home until late."

A shadow passes over his face when I look up at him.

"That's terrible."

Before he can say anything else, people surround us, and for the next two hours, I shake hands with person after person. There's no way I'll remember even a quarter of them, and frankly my face is sore from smiling. The sight of Nonno heading for us is a welcome distraction.

"Rachael, you look beautiful this evening," he says, reaching over to take my hand in his before placing a light kiss to the back. "Are you all settled in at the new place?"

"Yes, thank you, Nonno."

"I suppose one day soon Vonni will take you house hunting."

I knew Nonno's place wasn't permanent, so why am I so crestfallen at the thought of leaving? It's not my home. It's crazy to love everything about it, from the initials carved in the tree out front, to our evenings spent in the Jacuzzi tub.

Vonni's forehead wrinkles. "What's wrong, cara?"

"Nothing," I tell him, looking down at the reflection staring back at me from my beautiful gold pumps.

"You can tell us anything, my dear," Nonno says.

"I know we can't stay." Furiously, I brush away tears before they can fall, and I hate embarrassing myself like this in the middle of the engagement ball. "It's silly to be depressed at the thought of leaving."

"You are sentimental like my Raine." Nonno raises my chin with one finger. "She loved that old house. It's the reason I've kept it all these years. She would want you to stay." He looks at Vonni. "Do you want to live there?"

"I'll live anywhere Rachael wants to."

"It's settled then. The house is my wedding gift to you."

"Nonno, a house is too big of a gift," I object. "Can't I buy it from you?"

"Nonsense." He chuckles. "Now, if you want to do

something for me, you can fill it with a whole new generation of Morans."

I lean in to kiss his cheek. "It's a deal."

"Yes, well then," he says, stepping back with a blush on his cheeks.

He coughs into his hand before walking off and disappearing outside.

"Only you can make the great Giovanni Moran Senior blush," Vonni says with a shake of his head.

"Are you really ok with us living at Nonno's place?"

"Cara, you could have picked to live in a castle. Instead, you chose Nonno's old house for sentimental reasons. You're one of the few people that don't care about my family's money. It's one of the many reasons I fell in love with you."

We stand there in silence for a minute when a thought occurs to me.

"Where did Chantal go off to? Wonderful friend I am, leaving him in the lurch."

"My aunts have him in their clutches." Vonni laughs. "They are to keep him comfortable among the chaos. Let's go see if we can find him."

"That was really sweet of you to invite him," I tell him as we walk hand in hand. "He said you even sent the tux."

"I knew how crazy it was going to be." He smiles down at me. "I figured it would be nice for you to have your best friend here, besides Mandy."

When we go back outside, I notice most of the tables had been removed and Chantal is indeed holding court at a back table with Mandy and Vonni's aunts.

Elena turns to me and smiles. "So, you know everyone now, right?"

"Hardly. I wasn't thinking there would be that many people."

"Apparently, they're all sticking around as well. I went to the parking stand and asked how many people have left so far and he said only about twenty. John is holed up in his study, smoking cigars with Vito, Dom, Antonio, Frankie, and Marco."

I look around the tent, having lost sight of Vonni. The hair on the back of my neck stands up. Quickly, I excuse myself and set off toward the house. I mill around the outer edges of the crowd, scanning for a glimpse of his chestnut hair. Having no luck, I spot Christian's head above the crowd. When I get closer, I see he's surrounded by Sebastian, Rafe, Charlotte, Luke, and Johnny.

"Has anyone seen Vonni?"

"He snuck away for a minute," Christian says, pointing to a set of French doors behind them.

"Thanks, Christian."

The door opens onto a small, dimly lit terrace. Vonni stands at the railing, looking out into the side yard.

Coming up behind him, I run my hand along his back. "What are you doing out here?"

"I was hoping you'd come find me."

He turns, putting his arms around me.

"And why is that?"

I wrap my arms around his neck, ruffling the hair at his nape.

"I've been wanting to do this all night."

He leans down, sucking at my bottom lip and grabbing my butt. Palming my ass cheeks, he takes a wide stance so he can fit me tightly against his hard length. I can't help but moan into his mouth, moving my hands from his neck to his chest. The erratic beating of his heart is both a turn on and a comfort.

A crack rents the otherwise still night. Vonni's body jerks a second before his arms fall away. The shaman's words come back to me in a rush, and I run behind him as he's falling, catching him under the arms. I kick off my heels and steady him in my arms.

"Cara, leave me."

His voice maintains its commanding air despite the obvious pain he's in.

Ignoring him, I drag him backward toward the door.

"Go inside, leave me here," he hisses through his teeth.

"Shut up and let me work. We both know I'm not leaving you out here."

I bend over him, trying to shield his body with mine as best I can in case another shot is coming. The wire falls out of my cleavage, dropping onto the cement and I leave it there. Setting Vonni down gently, I reach behind me to open the door, grab him under his arms again, and lift him over the thresh hold. His soft grunt of pain lets me know he's still with me, even though he's no longer trying to order me around.

Sebastian's the first one to see me and comes running.

"Rachael, what happened?" he asks, dropping to the ground next to me.

"He's been shot!"

Now I have him safely inside, my whole body shakes.

"Christian, get over here!"

Everyone in the group comes running toward us as Vonni moans in pain while Sebastian runs a hand over his shoulder.

"I only heard one shot before Vonni fell." My voice quivers as I say, "I protected him as best as I could, fearing a second shot that never came."

Christian unbuttons his tux coat, removing a revolver from a holster and heads out the door with Johnny, Luke, and Rafe hot on his heels.

"I'm going to get John," Charlotte says, taking off at a run.

"Sebastian?"

My trembling hands are covered in Vonni's blood, and I need him to tell me what I can do for Vonni.

"Help me get his jacket off."

Sebastian looks down at my hands, then back at Vonni's closed eyes. His face scrunches up in pain as Sebastian gently raises him up, turning him so I can remove his tux jacket. With the jacket off, I can see where the blood's coming from. Tearing his dress shirt, I inspect the wound in his shoulder. Sebastian rolls Vonni toward him for me to check the back of

216

the wound.

"I see the exit wound, so I don't think the bullet is still in there."

Vonni opens his eyes and grabs Sebastian's arm. "Rachael."

"I'm still here, Vonni," I say, lightly touching his arm.

He visibly relaxes in my arms. "Are you hurt, cara?"

"No, love, I'm fine. You were the only one hurt. How bad is the pain?" My voice breaks. "Baby, I'm worried about the amount of blood you've lost."

"I'll be fine, cara. I'm a tough guy to kill." He takes a breath and groans. "I don't have use of my left arm at the moment. Seb, get me up. Where's Pop?"

"Charlotte took off to get him." Chewing my lip, I ask, "Baby, are you sure it's a good idea for you to be upright."

At Vonni's head nod, Sebastian lifts him up, letting Vonni lean on him for a second. Once he's standing, his gaze racks the length of my body, searching intently for any wounds.

"I'm fine, love," I assure him, stroking along his jaw with my hand.

"Fine." Sebastian smiles down at me. "Hell, she drug your ass in here to get help."

"I told her to leave me." Vonni rubs his thumb across my cheek. "Twice."

"Luck is on my side," I remind him, pointing down at his wolf ring.

"Never take that fucking ring off," Sebastian says.

"Oh, I won't. It could have been fatal instead of just a shoulder wound."

Charlotte comes running back toward us. "DJ caught the shooter. He's in John's office, but he won't talk."

Vonni and Sebastian exchange a long look.

"What's with the look?"

"Whoever shot Vonni either took the risk of being shot themselves, or they had permission." Sebastian lets out a long breath. "In which case, all our lives are in danger."

"Jesus Christ, Seb."

Vonni shoots Sebastian a glare before proceeding to look down at my chest.

"The only thing you're looking at is boobs. The stupid wire fell out while I was bent over you outside, and I left it. There's no way they didn't hear the shot, followed by nothing. I'm surprised the place isn't already crawling with FBI."

"I'll hold them off as long as I can," Charlotte says with a stubborn tilt to her chin.

Vonni takes off toward John's office with Sebastian and me hot on his heels. His stride's brisk despite the red still seeping through his dress shirt and his arm dangling limply at his side.

"Cara, you can't come in." Vonni stops short at the closed door. "Seb, stay out here with her."

At first, I'm shocked that Vonni went in and shut the door in my face. Then rage takes over, but Sebastian's quick to grab my arm when I go for the door handle.

"You don't want to be a part of what's happening in there."

"We're all in danger, I don't have a choice."

When I shove him aside and enter John's office, there's a man, beaten and bloody, strapped to a chair in front of the large oak desk. Men stand around the room staring at me.

Vonni steps toward us. "What the fuck did I say, Seb?"

Another wave of anger surges inside of me, the likes of which I have never experienced before.

"Fuck you. A man tried to kill you, could have gotten me, and now we're all in danger. I'm staying."

"She saved Vonni's life." Nonno moves from behind the man strapped to the chair. "She's more than proven her loyalty. She stays."

John threads his fingers together, nodding at my chest from behind his desk. When I shake my head no, he says nothing to contradict Nonno's order.

A man I've never seen before throws a punch at the guy strapped to the chair. Despite the sickening thud, he remains silent. Fear grips me. What if the FBI busts in the door and we have no answers? What if more of the Morans are shot as a result? Instinct takes over and, looking around the room, inspiration strikes. I grab the fire poker and thrust it into the fire.

"What are you doing?" Christian asks, a look of confusion on his face.

I nod at the man strapped to the chair. "Do we know who he is?"

"He's one of Vito's guys, Gus," John says. "The question is if the hit was approved or not."

"Gus, have you ever heard the story of King Edward II of England?"

I rotate the poker in the fire.

"What does he have to do with anything?"

He watches me closely out of the eye that's less swollen.

"I'm glad you ask. He was married to Princess Isabelle of France in order to broker peace between the two countries. The problem is that Edward was gay. His first lover was killed and for a time he turned to Isabelle and fathered the only children they would have. It was short-lived, though, because a young boy caught his eye. The boy had plans to increase his wealth and could easily manipulate Edward. For his lover, he took the queen's dowry and decreased her monthly living expenses. He stole land belonging to the barons and gave it to his lover."

"A baron became the queen's lover and vowed to gain his lands back. Many years later, he did just that. King Edward died in jail. Rumor was that he killed Edward by sticking a hot fire poker inside him. It was never confirmed because the wound was immediately cauterized."

"You aren't going to stick a hot poker in my mouth," Gus sputters.

"You're right I'm not." I look at Christian. "Untie him from the chair, pull down his pants, and put him face down across the desk."

All the men in the room look back and forth at each other.

"Do as she asks," John commands. "If a hot poker doesn't make him talk, nothing will."

As they untie him, his eyes grow as big as saucers, and he looks at John. "You're not really going to let her do it, are you?"

"That's up to you, Gus."

The guys get as far as bending him over the desk before he cracks.

"Vito ordered the hit. I was supposed to take out both John and Vonni, but I could never get a bead on John." He looks in my direction. "I had a perfect shot at Vonni before she came outside. I had no choice but to shoot around her. Vito told me if I did this, he'd make me a capo. Nobody was supposed to know he was making a move against the Morans."

Setting the poker back in its place, I let out a relieved breath.

"Would you really have done it?" Gus asks me as they stand him up.

I walk up to him and stand close, looking him in the eye. "If you had killed anyone in my family, you'd be begging me for the poker instead of what I would have done to you."

"DJ and Johnny get all the bosses out," John orders. "We don't have long before the FBI is up our asses."

Once they are out the door, he turns to Christian. "You're in charge of Gus until his fate is decided. Please try to keep the feds from getting their hands on him."

Christian drags a whimpering Gus out the door as John turns to the rest of the men. "Everyone else, get as many of the guests out as you can."

"Thank you, Rachael." Nonno kisses my hand before turning to John. "I'm going after Vito."

John gets up and walks over to me, swiftly drawing me into his arms. "You not only saved my son, but you probably saved the rest of us." He leans back and looks into my eyes. "Anything you desire is yours."

"I would do anything to save my family. There's nothing I

need that I don't already have."

He smiles down at me before turning on his heel and walking out. When Vonni tries to approach me, I hold up my hand to stop him before I run from the room. Tears mar my vision as I open doors looking for a bathroom. Finally finding one, I shut and lock the door before bending over the toilet and heaving. When there's nothing left, I sob and shake, sinking onto the floor. Hugging myself, I curl into as tight of a ball as my dress will allow.

THIRTY-SEVEN

VONNI

Rachael thinks she can just hold a hand up and that will keep me from going after her? Hardly. I may not be as good as DJ, but I can certainly follow Rachael without her knowing it. Not that she'd see me through the tears streaming down her face.

From the other side of the bathroom door, I can hear her violently retching. It takes everything in me to give her a few minutes of privacy. If I try to comfort her before she's willing to let me, I'll only anger her. After seeing what she can do with a fire poker, I have no desire to piss her off. Here I stand with my head resting against the door, waiting.

From inside, I hear shuffling, then sobbing. My right hand curls into a fist so tight it hurts. My left arm is slowly getting the feeling back, but I wish it was still numb. This feels like true torture. I'd take physical torment any day over this. Her pain is a raw and festering wound inside of me. It's my fault. My world has taken this beautifully innocent spirit and put a black mark on it. There is nothing I can do to change that, and I'm too much of a heartless bastard to let her go. Nonno is right. She's more than strong enough to handle our world. Her actions today have proven that. The only thing left to do is pick the lock and remind her of who she is.

Opening the door, I see her curled into a ball. When she lifts her tear-streaked face, it's like a punch to the gut. I sink to the floor next to her and try to lift her onto my lap with only one arm working properly and a sharp jab of pain takes my breath away for a minute. No matter how hard I try to keep my pain from her, I know it's written all over my face. My shoulder hurts like a bitch, and pinpricks now skate down my right arm. She buries her head into what's left of my shirt and hiccups.

I rain kisses over the top of her silky hair as I promise, "Cara, I'll never underestimate you again,"

"I thought you might die, and there wasn't a damn thing I could do to stop it. Then I went into a rage at the thought the danger wasn't over, and everyone could be killed. I went off instinct, but it cost me emotionally."

"You held yourself together when you needed to. You are the bravest, most beautiful woman. I'm the luckiest bastard on the planet." I cup her face, kissing away her tears. If I could take away her pain with my lips, I would. "Cara, let's go home."

"Not so fast, you two," Kyle says from the doorway with his arms crossed over his massive chest. He looks at Rachael and holds up the wire. "Why did I find this on the ground outside?"

"Listen, Kyle." Her eyes flash, and she drags out each syllable of his name. "I've had a really shitty day. You're the one that put it in my cleavage without taping it down. What did you think was going to happen when I bent over?"

"Are you giving me lip right now? I should haul your ass in!"

"Don't piss her off," I warn him behind a cough.

"I'll get to you in a second," Kyle says, sending a murderous glance my way.

"You will do no such thing."

Rachael leaps off my lap to stand toe-to-toe with Kyle.

A muscle in Kyle's jaw ticks. "Yeah, and why would that be?"

"While under your protection, I was almost killed."

Her defiant glare would have made a lesser man flinch.

"Happens all the time."

He dares to look at her like he's bored. When I look at Rachael, I can tell that only pisses her off even more.

"Fine. You're messing with the wrong girl today, Kyle." She looks down at her nails as if she's uninterested in what he has to say. "I wonder if Fields would be interested to know the taxpayers are funding your love life?"

"What the fuck are you talking about?" he asks, his voice goes up a couple of octaves.

"You should be more discreet." I can't tell what she's got up her sleeve but judging by the Grinch like grin she has on her face, it must be good. "Agent Keller's shirt was on backward when I got in the van earlier tonight."

"I told you not to piss her off."

Only my fucking girl pulls a rabbit like that out of her hat.

"You're lying," he spits out, his face turning a disturbing shade of purple.

"Is that so?" She fishes her cell phone out of her dress. She unlocks it, scrolling until she finds what she's looking for. "I think you'll find this picture of agent Keller . . . illuminating."

She takes a few steps back from him and holds up her phone. When he tries to wrench the phone out of her hand, she's one step ahead of him, holding it just out of reach.

"Why you . . ."

He takes a menacing step toward Rachael. Bad move. Nobody threatens my girl and gets away with it. I'm on my feet, bad arm, and all. With lightning speed, I remove my gun from its holster and move around Rachael. Thankfully, my injuries are on the opposite side of my body because I don't shoot as well with my other hand.

"Lay a finger on her and I'll drop you where you stand."
I press the gun against his temple so he can tell I mean business. He gives me a defiant glare until I cock it. "Try me."

"Fine," Kyle says, through gritted teeth. He stares at Rachael as he asks, "What are you proposing in exchange for making that photo disappear?"

I lower my gun, but I'm not foolish enough to holster it just yet. Watching Kyle out of the corner of my eye, I wait to hear what terms Rachael has in mind.

"Leave the family alone, at least for today." Her smile holds no hint of mirth. "You can always come for us later."

"You can count on it."

Calmly, he backs out of the bathroom and walks down the hall.

THIRTY-EIGHT

RACHAEL

"Ray . . . psst . . . Ray, are you down there?" Chantal whispers from the opposite end of the hallway.

"Yeah, the coast is clear," I whisper back from the bathroom doorway. "It's just Vonni and me."

Chantal peeks around the corner before proceeding with Charlotte and Mandy hot on his heels. I motion all of them into the massive bathroom.

"Did Agent Fitzsimmons find you?" Mandy asks, a frown clear on her face.

"He did." Vonni chuckles. "Cara took care of him. For today anyway."

Chantal gives me a sideways glance. "You go on with your bad self."

"We held them off as long as we could," Charlotte says, looking around nervously.

Vonni runs a hand over his face. "I was wondering what took them so long."

"They may have had some trouble at the gate."

Chantal looks back and forth between Charlotte and Mandy.

"Do tell, I could use a laugh about now."

"Sam was needed elsewhere, so we took over." Excitement lights his eyes. "We locked ourselves in the guard shack and pretended not to know how to work anything, even though Sam gave us a quick tutorial. Finally, the agents climbed the fence. Wouldn't you know it's an electric fence?"

He shrugs, a wicked gleam in his eye. "The three of us couldn't figure out how to shut it down."

Mandy giggles. "From inside the booth, we couldn't hear them either."

Vonni laughs. "I'm never fucking with any of you."

"Do you know if everyone got out?" I ask, chewing on my lip.

"I took care of it." Everyone turns to look at DJ standing in the doorway. "You three bought us enough time to sneak everyone out the back way. Fields is really pissed. He and John are still going at it in John's office."

"Vonni, you still need stitches."

I look down at the slow trickle of blood coming from his shoulder. His arm no longer lays limp against his side, but I can tell he's favoring it.

"Come on." DJ looks up and down the hallway before motioning with two fingers. "Stay right behind me."

He veers off in the direction that Chantal just came from and all of us follow closely behind. When he comes to the corner, he sticks his head out before continuing down another dimly lit hallway. Slowly opening the terrace door, he looks around, listening. The night is silent and still.

"Mandy, take Vonni and go first," DJ whispers. "Once you hit the tree line, go to the fort we had as kids. Johnny will wait for you there."

"I won't go without Rachael," Vonni whispers back.

"Vonni, don't be silly, you're injured." I kiss him quickly on the mouth. "I'll be right behind you."

He gives me a brief nod before he and Mandy clear the wrought iron railing, taking off at a dead run for the tree line a few yards away. The night remains still and calm.

"The rest of you don't stop for anything, I'm right behind you."

"What about Marco?" Charlotte asks, hesitating.

"If I don't make sure you get home safely, he's threatened to cut off a part of me that really needs to stay attached."

Charlotte gives DJ a nod. Helping each other over the railing, I grab Charlotte and Chantal's hands as we take off running. At the tree line, DJ passes us, taking the lead. He walks at a brisk pace, easily navigating the woods at night. Not caring how he does it, I concentrate on not falling.

A car's headlights flash up ahead, catching my attention. Suddenly I'm nervous. What if it's a trap? Tugging on my hand, Charlotte pulls me toward either salvation or hell, I'm not sure which yet. The woods fall away to reveal a clearing and a lone figure stands next to a long, sleek, dark-colored car.

"Hurry and get in."

Sebastian's husky voice is such a relief that my knees almost buckle. He opens the door and pulls the seat forward. Charlotte ducks under Sebastian's arm and crawls in and I follow her, scooting over to make room for Chantal to squeeze in. DJ runs around and hops in the passenger seat as Sebastian sets the car in motion. The tires spin a second in the grass before they catch.

"Everyone buckle up, there's a dirt road ahead, so it's going to be bumpy."

"Sebastian, did you see Vonni and Mandy?" I ask, after getting myself buckled.

"Johnny has them." He looks at me in the rearview mirror and smiles. "You didn't think I'd leave you behind? You forget, I've seen what your crazy ass does with a fire poker."

From the passenger seat, DJ laughs so hard he snorts.

"It looks like we aren't the only ones who've had quite an evening," Chantal says, leaning over me to look at Charlotte.

"I may have threatened one of Vito's guys with a fire poker." Looking at Chantal, I shrug. "I may have also blackmailed an FBI agent."

"She put it in the fire, threatening to stick that shit up his ass." DJ leans over the front seat, a big grin on his face. "I love your crazy ass. You and Vonni are perfect for each other."

"You have been a busy girl," Chantal says, making a tsking sound.

"It wasn't my proudest moment, DJ, but he shot Vonni. He wasn't talking, and I knew it was only a matter of time before the FBI descended on the place."

"I'm sorry about that." DJ's smile fades away, a troubled look replacing it. "Nonno's had me following Vonni since you told him about the threat. I was walking the tree line while he was on the veranda. Unfortunately, Gus was so well hidden I didn't see him, only the flash of the muzzle from his gun. I could catch him, but not quickly enough."

"You can't stop everything, DJ." I meet his gaze with all sincerity. "I'm grateful. Without your interference, he'd have shot off more rounds, killing both Vonni and me."

Silence fills the car for a few minutes. Sebastian meets my eyes for a second in the rearview mirror before turning his attention to the dirt road ahead.

"Tell me about blackmailing an FBI agent."

"Kyle . . . what an asshat."

"Ray, I've never heard you curse before," Chantal says, having the nerve to look impressed.

"He threatened to take me in for losing my wire outside. He's the one who never taped the thing down."

"Wait a minute," Charlotte interrupts. "You were wearing a wire tonight?"

"The FBI grabbed me a few weeks ago and John thought it would be better to play along."

"Back to Kyle," Sebastian prompts.

"When I got in the van for them to fit me for the wire, agent Keller was with him. I noticed she had her shirt on backward. Discreetly, I took a picture with my phone. I thought that kind of leverage might come in handy. I didn't expect to have to use it so soon."

"Damn, I'm never pissing you off," DJ says, turning back around.

"It bought the Morans a reprieve for the day, but Fitzsimmons will be out for blood now. Especially after Vonni pulled a gun on him."

Sebastian turns onto a paved road and asks, "You still have that photo?"

"Of course."

"Text it to me and my guy on the inside will handle Fitzsimmons."

Charlotte pouts. "Why didn't I know about this whole wire thing?"

DJ looks over his shoulder at her and smiles. "Char, we love you, but you're not good at keeping secrets."

"Where are we going, Sebastian?" I ask, watching the trees flash by Chantal's window.

"I'm bringing everyone home. You'll be my first stop. Vonni won't rest until you're with him. Doc should have at least started to patch him up by the time we get there."

"I'll get out with Ray to save you a trip," Chantal says to Sebastian. He turns to me and grabs my hand. "Just in case you need help with Vonni."

Squeezing his hand to show my appreciation, I lay my head back against the leather seat and shut my eyes.

THIRTY-NINE

VONNI

Rachael's phone chirps from her nightstand beside the bed and she leans over, feeling for it. When it falls to the floor with a thud, I hear a string of curse words. My girl has spent too much time around me and that thought brings a smile to my face.

Turning onto my back, I try to cross my arms behind my head, but the wrapping around my shoulder won't let me. I'll have to settle for propping myself up on pillows with my arms by my side. From the floor, I hear her answer the phone as she crawls onto the bed.

"And you call me at"—she looks over at the clock on the bedside table—"six in the morning to tell me this?"

"Who is it, cara?"

Despite her question about the hour of the call, she doesn't seem the least bit annoyed with the caller.

"My grandmother."

She rolls her eyes and pushes a button, setting the phone on her lap.

"You're on speaker," Rachael tells her.

"The vision I had involves both of you." Her level of excitement is such that I picture an announcer from *The Price Is Right*. "Are you sitting down?"

"It's six o'clock in the morning. We're still in bed, Grandma." Rachael chews on her nail. "What's up?"

"I saw a little girl, around the age of four, with long dark hair and dark blue eyes. She giggles, running as hard as she can through the forest. It's a game she's playing. Two adolescent wolves with chestnut fur hang back for a time, to make her think she's going to win. One of them suddenly leaps through the air to land on her back, bringing her down. Licking her neck, he nips her hair before letting her up."

"Who is the little girl?" I ask her grandmother.

She laughs. "Your daughter, of course."

"Our daughter runs with wolves?"

I'm skeptical about this scenario, even though I trust in her visions.

"You are very frustrating." She lets out an impatient sigh. "In my first vision, I saw a chestnut wolf that turned out to be you. The adolescent wolves in my vision are obviously your sons."

"Shit."

I sit up and try to pull air into my lungs, feeling like the winds just been knocked out of me.

Her laughter fills the room, then the line goes dead. Rachael and I sit there staring at each other for a long time. Memories of us play like a highlight reel in my head and one particular memory stays with me, snapping me out of my stupor.

"On our first date, you said you wanted three kids." I move closer, rubbing my facial hair along the side of her neck. When I reach her ear, I whisper into it, "I admit I hadn't given it much thought before now. We should probably get started, don't you think?"

She lovingly runs her hand along the side of my face and,

turning toward me, she presses her lips against mine. The kiss quickly turns hungry, and I press her back into the soft mattress. I find I'm looking forward to this latest vision of her grandmother's coming true.

Thank you for reading.

If you enjoyed This Thing of Ours, please consider leaving a review. When readers take the time to leave a star rating or write-up on **Amazon** or **Goodreads**, it means the world to me. I'm always telling my family and friends about the sweet comments you guys leave!

Become a member of my VIP Club by signing up here.

Members get exclusive sneak peeks and freebies, release updates, and more!

About the Author

Gladys Cross writes steamy and morally gray contemporary romances.

Her heroes are damaged, heartbroken, sometimes not all the way sane, and heart-stoppingly drool worthy.

She's not afraid to tackle the mafia, bikers, your common criminal, vampires, werewolves, or even the devil himself.

When she isn't dipping her toe into the darker side of love, she converts into mom mode. She's not above instigating water gun fights, but her favorite pastime is beating her daughter and husband in a game of cards.

gladysafterdark.com